The Village Institute (where the party was held)

The Playing Field

(where the Fête was held)

The Blacksmith's Cottage   The Forge

The Postman's Cottage

Mr Blunt's Corn Shop (where Billy Blunt lives)

Mr Smale's Grocer's shop

Short cut to School

Miss Muggins Shop (where Jilly lives)

Bakery   Mrs Hubble's Baker's shop (where Mrs & Miss Bloss live)

Cross Roads

To the Town (where the Market is)

The School

GIRLS   BOYS

Teacher's Cottage

VILLAGE

THE
MILLY-
MOLLY-
MANDY
STORYBOOK

KINGFISHER
LONDON & NEW YORK

Publisher's Note

*The stories in this collection are reproduced in the form in which they appeared
upon first publication in the U.K. by George G. Harrap & Co. Ltd.
All spellings remain consistent with these original editions.*

The stories in this collection first appeared in
Milly-Molly-Mandy Stories (1928), *More of Milly-Molly-Mandy* (1929),
Further Doings of Milly-Molly-Mandy (1932), *Milly-Molly-Mandy Again* (1948)
published by George G. Harrap & Co. Ltd.

Published in the United States by Kingfisher,
175 Fifth Ave., New York, NY 10010
Kingfisher is an imprint of Macmillan Children's Books, London.
All rights reserved.

Distributed in the U.S. and Canada by Macmillan,
175 Fifth Ave., New York, NY 10010

Library of Congress Cataloging-in-Publication data has been applied for.

ISBN: 978-0-7534-5332-2

Kingfisher books are available for special promotions and premiums. For details contact:
Special Markets Department, Macmillan, 175 Fifth Avenue, New York, NY 10010.

For more information, please visit www.kingfisherbooks.com

Printed and bound by CPI Group (UK) Ltd., Croydon, CR0 4YY

25 24 23

THE
MILLY-
MOLLY-
MANDY
STORYBOOK

KINGFISHER
NEW YORK

CONTENTS

1

MILLY-MOLLY-MANDY
GOES ERRANDS

ONCE UPON A TIME there was a little girl.

She had a Father, and a Mother, and a
Grandpa, and a Grandma, and an Uncle, and
an Aunty; and they all lived together in a nice
white cottage with a thatched roof.

This little girl had short hair, and short legs,
and short frocks (pink-and-white-striped cotton in summer, and red serge in winter). But
her name wasn't short at all. It was Millicent
Margaret Amanda. But Father and Mother
and Grandpa and Grandma and Uncle and
Aunty couldn't very well call out "Millicent
Margaret Amanda!" every time they wanted
her, so they shortened it to 'Milly-Molly-
Mandy,' which is quite easy to say.

Now everybody in the nice white cottage

with the thatched roof had some particular job to do – even Milly-Molly-Mandy.

Father grew vegetables in the big garden by the cottage. Mother cooked the dinners and did the washing. Grandpa took the vegetables to market in his little pony-cart. Grandma knitted socks and mittens and nice warm woollies for them all. Uncle kept cows (to give them milk) and chickens (to give them eggs). Aunty sewed frocks and shirts for them, and did the sweeping and dusting.

And Milly-Molly-Mandy, what did she do?

Well, Milly-Molly-Mandy's legs were short, as I've told you, but they were very lively, just right for running errands. So Milly-Molly-Mandy was quite busy, fetching and carrying things, and taking messages.

One fine day Milly-Molly-Mandy was in the garden playing with Toby the dog, when Father poked his head out from the other side of a big row of beans, and said:

"Milly-Molly-Mandy, run down to Mr

Moggs' cottage and ask for the trowel he borrowed from me!"

So Milly-Molly-Mandy said, "Yes, Farver!"
and ran in to get her hat.

At the kitchen door was Mother, with a basket
of eggs in her hand. And when she saw Milly-
Molly-Mandy she said:

"Milly-Molly-Mandy, run down to Mrs
Moggs and give her these eggs. She's got visitors."

So Milly-Molly-Mandy said, "Yes, Muvver!"
and took the basket. "Trowel for Farver, eggs
for Muvver," she thought to herself.

Then Grandpa came up and said:

"Milly-Molly-Mandy, please get me a ball of
string from Miss Muggins' shop – here's a
penny."

So Milly-Molly-Mandy said, "Yes,
Grandpa!" and took the penny, thinking to
herself, "Trowel for Farver, eggs for Muvver,
string for Grandpa."

As she passed through the kitchen Grandma,
who was sitting in her armchair knitting said:

"Milly-Molly-Mandy, will you get me a skein
of red wool? Here's a sixpence."

So Milly-Molly-Mandy said, "Yes, Grandma!" and took the sixpence. "Trowel for Farver, eggs for Muvver, string for Grandpa, red wool for Grandma," she whispered over to herself.

As she went into the passage Uncle came striding up in a hurry.

"Oh, Milly-Molly-Mandy," said Uncle, "run like a good girl to Mr Blunt's shop, and tell him I'm waiting for the chicken-feed he promised to send!"

So Milly-Molly-Mandy said, "Yes, Uncle!" and thought to herself, "Trowel for Farver, eggs for Muvver, string for Grandpa, red wool for Grandma, chicken-feed for Uncle."

As she got her hat off the peg Aunty called from the parlour where she was dusting:

"Is that Milly-Molly-Mandy? Will you get me a packet of needles, dear? Here's a penny!"

So Milly-Molly-Mandy said, "Yes, Aunty!" and took the penny, thinking to herself, "Trowel for Farver, eggs for Muvver, string for Grandpa, red wool for Grandma, chicken-feed for Uncle, needles for Aunty, and I do hope there won't be anything more!"

GRANDPA · GRANDMA · FATHER · MOTHER · UNCLE · AUNTY · MILLY-MOLLY-MANDY.

But there was nothing else, so Milly-Molly-Mandy started out down the path. When she came to the gate Toby the dog capered up, looking very excited at the thought of a walk. But Milly-Molly-Mandy eyed him solemnly, and said:

"Trowel for Farver, eggs for Muvver, string for Grandpa, red wool for Grandma, chicken-feed for Uncle, needles for Aunty. No, Toby, you mustn't come now, I've too much to think about. But I promise to take you for a walk when I come back!"

So she left Toby on the other side of the gate, and set off down the road, with the basket and the pennies and the sixpence.

Presently she met a little friend, and the little friend said:

"Hello, Milly-Molly-Mandy! I've got a new see-saw! Do come on it with me!"

But Milly-Molly-Mandy looked at her solemnly and said:

"Trowel for Farver, eggs for Muvver, string for Grandpa, red wool for Grandma, chicken-feed for Uncle, needles for Aunty. No, Susan, I can't come now, I'm busy. But I'd like to come

12

when I get back – after I've taken Toby for a walk."

So Milly-Molly-Mandy went on her way with the basket and the pennies and the six-pence.

Soon she came to the Moggs' cottage.

"Please, Mrs Moggs, can I have the trowel for Farver? And here are some eggs from Muvver!" she said.

Mrs Moggs was very much obliged indeed for the eggs, and fetched the trowel and a piece of seed-cake for Milly-Molly-Mandy's own self. And Milly-Molly-Mandy went on her way with the empty basket.

Next she came to Miss Muggins' little shop.

"Please, Miss Muggins, can I have a ball of string for Grandpa and a skein of red wool for Grandma?"

So Miss Muggins put the string and the wool into Milly-Molly-Mandy's basket, and took a penny and a sixpence in exchange. So that left Milly-Molly-Mandy with one penny. And Milly-Molly-Mandy couldn't remember what that penny was for.

"Sweeties, perhaps?" said Miss Muggins,

glancing at the row of glass bottles on the shelf.

But Milly-Molly-Mandy shook her head.

"No," she said, "and it can't be chicken-feed for Uncle, because that would be more than a penny, only I haven't got to pay for it."

"It must be sweeties!" said Miss Muggins.

"No," said Milly-Molly-Mandy, "but I'll remember soon. Good morning, Miss Muggins!"

So Milly-Molly-Mandy went on to Mr Blunt's and gave him Uncle's message, and then she sat down on the doorstep and thought what that penny could be for.

And she couldn't remember.

But she remembered one thing: "It's for Aunty," she thought, "and I love Aunty." And she thought for just a little while longer. Then suddenly she sprang up and went back to Miss Muggins' shop.

"I've remembered!" she said. "It's needles for Aunty!"

So Miss Muggins put the packet of needles into the basket, and took the penny, and Milly-Molly-Mandy set off for home.

"That's a good little messenger to remember all those things!" said Mother, when she got there. They were just going to begin dinner. "I thought you were only going with my eggs!"

"She went for my trowel!" said Father.

"And my string!" said Grandpa.

"And my wool!" said Grandma.

"And my chicken-feed!" said Uncle.

"And my needles!" said Aunty.

Then they all laughed; and Grandpa, feeling in his pocket, said:

"Well, here's another errand for you – go and get yourself some sweeties!"

So after dinner Toby had a nice walk and his mistress got her sweets. And then Milly-Molly-Mandy and little-friend-Susan had a lovely time on the see-saw, chatting and eating raspberry-drops, and feeling very happy and contented indeed.

2

MILLY-MOLLY-MANDY
SPENDS A PENNY

ONCE UPON A TIME Milly-Molly-Mandy
found a penny in the pocket of an old coat.

Milly-Molly-Mandy felt very rich indeed.

She thought of all the things she could buy
with it, and there were so many that she did
not know which to choose. (That is the worst
of a penny). So Milly-Molly-Mandy asked
everybody with whom she lived, in the nice
white cottage with the thatched roof, what
they would do with it if they were her.

"Put it in the bank," said Grandpa promptly.
He was making up accounts. Milly-Molly-
Mandy thought that a good idea.

"Buy a skein of rainbow wool and learn to
knit," said Grandma, who was knitting by the
kitchen door. Milly-Molly-Mandy thought that
a good idea.

16

"Buy some seeds and grow mustard-and-cress," said Father, who was gardening. Milly-Molly-Mandy thought that quite a good idea.

"Buy a little patty-pan and make a cake in it," said Mother, who was cooking. Milly-Molly-Mandy thought that a very good idea.

"Save it up until you get three, and I'll let you buy a baby duckling with them," said Uncle, who was scooping out corn for his chickens. Milly-Molly-Mandy thought that an excellent idea.

"Get some sweets," said Aunty, who was very busy sewing, and did not want to be interrupted. Milly-Molly-Mandy thought that a very pleasant idea.

Then she went to her own little corner of the garden for a 'think', for she still could not make up her mind which of all those nice things to do. She thought and thought for a long time.

And then – what do you think she bought?

Some mustard-and-cress seeds, which she planted in a shallow box of earth and stood in a nice warm place by the tool-shed.

She watered it every day, and shaded it if the

sun were too hot; and at last the little seeds grew into a lovely clump of fresh green mustard-and-cress, that made you quite long for some bread and butter to eat it with.

When it was ready to cut Milly-Molly-Mandy went to Mrs Moggs, their neighbour down the road, who sometimes had summer visitors.

"Mrs Moggs," said Milly-Molly-Mandy, "if you should want some mustard-and-cress for your visitors' tea I have some to sell. It's very good, and quite cheap."

"Why, Milly-Molly-Mandy," said Mrs Moggs, "that's exactly what I am wanting! Is it ready for cutting now?"

So Milly-Molly-Mandy ran home and borrowed a pair of scissors and a little basket, and she snipped that lovely clump of fresh green mustard-and-cress (all but a tiny bit for her own tea) and carried it to Mrs Moggs.

And Mrs Moggs gave her two pence for it.

So Milly-Molly-Mandy had done one of the nice things and spent her penny, and now she had two pence!

Then Milly-Molly-Mandy took one of the pennies to the little village shop, and bought a skein of beautiful rainbow wool.

"Grandma," she said, when she got home, "please will you teach me to knit a kettle-holder?"

So Grandma found some knitting-needles and showed Milly-Molly-Mandy how to knit. And though it had to be undone several times at first, Milly-Molly-Mandy really did knit quite a nice kettle-holder, and there was just enough wool for it.

When she had put a loop in one corner to hang it up by she went to Mother, who was just putting the potatoes on to boil.

"Mother," said Milly-Molly-Mandy, "would you think this kettle-holder worth a penny?"

"Why, Milly-Molly-Mandy," said Mother,

Milly-Molly-Mandy finds a penny

"that is exactly what I am wanting, for my old one is all worn out! But the penny only pays for the wool, so you are making me a present of all your trouble." And Mother gave Milly-Molly-Mandy a penny and a kiss, and Milly-Molly-Mandy felt well paid.

So Milly-Molly-Mandy had done another of the nice things, had spent her penny, and learnt to knit, and still she had her penny!

Then Milly-Molly-Mandy took her penny down to the little village shop and bought a shiny tin patty-pan. And next baking-day Mother let her make a little cake in the patty-pan and put it in the oven. And it was such a beautiful little cake, and so nicely browned, that it seemed almost too good to eat.

Milly-Molly-Mandy put it outside on the window-sill to cool.

Presently, along came a lady cyclist, and as it was a very hot day she stopped at the nice white cottage with the thatched roof, and asked Milly-Molly-Mandy's Mother if she could have a glass of milk. And while she was drinking it she saw the little cake on the window-sill, and the little cake looked so good that the lady cyclist felt hungry and asked if she could have that too.

Milly-Molly-Mandy's Mother looked at Milly-Molly-Mandy, and Milly-Molly-Mandy gave a little gulp, and said "Yes." And the lady cyclist ate up the little patty-cake. And she did enjoy it!

When she had gone Milly-Molly-Mandy's Mother took up the pennies the lady cyclist had put on the table for the milk and the cake, and she gave one to Milly-Molly-Mandy because it was her cake.

So Milly-Molly-Mandy had done yet another of the nice things and spent her penny, but still she had her penny.

Then Milly-Molly-Mandy took her penny down to the little village shop and bought some sweets, lovely big aniseed balls, that changed colour as you sucked them.

She would not eat one until she got home, and then gave one to Grandpa and one to Grandma and one to Father and one to Mother and one to Uncle and one to Aunty. And then she found there were six for herself, so she ate them, and they were very nice.

So Milly-Molly-Mandy had done another of the nice things and spent her penny. But she still had one penny from the mustard-and-cress.

Then she went to Grandpa, and asked him please to put it in the bank for her.

And then she went to Uncle.

"Uncle," said Milly-Molly-Mandy, "I've done everything with my penny that everybody said, but you. And though I can't buy a little baby duckling yet, I've got a penny saved towards it, in the bank."

And it was not very long before Milly-Molly-Mandy had saved up to three pence; and then Uncle let her have a little yellow baby duckling all for her own.

3

MILLY-MOLLY-MANDY MEETS
HER GREAT-AUNT

ONCE UPON A TIME, one fine evening,
Milly-Molly-Mandy and her Father and
Mother and Grandpa and Grandma and Uncle
and Aunty were all sitting at supper (there was
bread-and-butter and cheese for the grown-
ups, and bread-and-milk for Milly-Molly-
Mandy, and baked apples and cocoa for them
all), when suddenly there came a loud bang-
bang! on the knocker.

"Run, Milly-Molly-Mandy," said Mother.
"That sounds like the postman!"

So Milly-Molly-Mandy jumped down from
her chair in a great hurry and fetched the letter, which was for Mother. Then she climbed
on her chair again, and everyone looked interested while Mother opened it.

It was from someone who called Milly-Molly-Mandy's Mother "Dear Polly," and was to ask if that someone might spend a few days with them, and it finished up, "Your affectionate Aunt Margaret."

Father and Mother and Grandpa and Grandma and Uncle and Aunty were quite pleased, and Milly-Molly-Mandy was pleased too, although she did not know who it was until Grandma said to her, "It is my sister Margaret, your great-aunty, who is coming." Then Milly-Molly-Mandy was very interested indeed.

"Is she my great-aunty and your sister too?" she asked Grandma.

"Yes, and she's my sister-in-law," said Grandpa.

"And my aunty," said Mother.

"And my aunty-in-law," said Father.

"And my aunty-in-law too," said Aunty.

"And my aunty," said Uncle.

25

"That sounds like the postman!"

"Fancy!" said Milly-Molly-Mandy. "She's all that, and she's a great-aunty too! I would like to see her!"

The next day Milly-Molly-Mandy helped Mother make up the spare room bed.

"I could wish the spare room were a little bigger," said Mother, and Milly-Molly-Mandy looked around gravely, and thought it really was rather small for a great-aunty. But she went and fetched some marigolds from her own little garden, and put them in a vase on the chest of drawers, for she knew there was lots of room for love, even if there was not much for great-aunties.

Then Milly-Molly-Mandy helped Father bring the big armchair out of the best parlour into the room where they always sat. Milly-Molly-Mandy was glad it was such a big chair – it really looked quite large enough even for a great-aunty.

Then Mother cooked some big fruit cakes and some little seed cakes and some sponge cakes and a whole lot of other things, and Milly-Molly-Mandy (who helped to clean up the cooking bowls and spoons) supposed a great-aunty must take quite a lot of feeding.

As soon as ever the last bowl was scraped Milly-Molly-Mandy ran down the road to tell little-friend-Susan the news.

Little-friend-Susan was walking on the wall, but she jumped down as soon as she saw Milly-Molly-Mandy.

"Oh, Susan!" said Milly-Molly-Mandy, "you know my Aunty?"

"Yes," said little-friend-Susan.

"Well," said Milly-Molly-Mandy, "she's just a usual aunty, but I've got a great-aunty coming to stay with us!"

Little-friend-Susan, being a best friend, was just as interested as Milly-Molly-Mandy, and it was soon settled that next morning she should come and play in Milly-Molly-Mandy's garden, so that she might see Great-Aunty Margaret for herself.

Then Milly-Molly-Mandy ran back home to dinner.

After dinner Mother and Grandma and Aunty and Milly-Molly-Mandy hurried through the washing-up, and tidied the cottage, while Father put the pony in the trap.

And then they changed their dresses, while Father drove to the station.

And then Milly-Molly-Mandy, in her clean frock, kept running to the gate to see if the pony-trap were in sight yet.

And at last it was – and Milly-Molly-Mandy was so excited that she raced into the cottage and jumped up and down, and then she ran out to the gate again, and opened it wide.

The pony trotted up to the gate and stopped, and Father got down first. And then he took down Great-Aunty Margaret's great basket. And then he helped down Great-Aunty Margaret her own self!

And what do you think Great-Aunty Margaret was like?

She was a little, little, white-haired lady, in a black bonnet and dress spotted with little mauve flowers, and she had a kind little face with pink cheeks.

Milly-Molly-Mandy was so surprised, it was

all she could do to mind her manners and not stare.

Great-Aunty Margaret was soon seated in the great armchair, and instead of filling it, as Milly-Molly-Mandy had expected, why – there was heaps of room for Milly-Molly-Mandy there too! And instead of eating up all the big fruit cakes and the little seed cakes and the sponge cakes and other things, there was lots for everybody in the family, including Milly-Molly-Mandy.

And as for the spare room being too small, it looked almost big, because Great-Aunty Margaret was such a little lady.

When Great-Aunty Margaret saw the flowers on her chest of drawers she said gently:

"Why, Millicent Margaret Amanda, I believe that is your doing! Thank you, my dearie!"

"Oh, Great-Aunty Margaret!" said Milly-Molly-Mandy, reaching to kiss her again. "I do like you! Would you mind if I showed you to Susan this evening, instead of making her wait till tomorrow?"

4

MILLY-MOLLY-MANDY
GOES BLACKBERRYING

ONCE UPON A TIME Milly-Molly-Mandy found some big ripe blackberries on her way home from school. There were six great beauties and one little hard one, so Milly-Molly-Mandy put the little hard one in her mouth and carried the others home on a leaf.

She gave one to Father, and Father said, "Ah! That makes me think the time for blackberry puddings has come!"

Then she gave one to Mother, and asked what it made her think of. And Mother said, "A whole row of pots of blackberry jam that I ought to have in my store-cupboard!"

Then she gave one to Grandpa, and Grandpa said it made him think "Blackberry tart!"

And Grandma said, "Blackberry jelly!"

And Uncle said, "Stewed blackberry-and-apple!"

And Aunty said, "A plate of blackberries with sugar and cream!"

"My!" thought Milly-Molly-Mandy, as she threw away the empty leaf, "I must get a big, big basket and go blackberrying the very next Saturday, so that there can be lots of puddings and jam and tarts and jelly and stewed blackberry-and-apple and fresh blackberries, for Farver and Muvver and Grandpa and Grandma and Uncle and Aunty – and me! I'll ask Susan to come too."

So the very next Saturday Milly-Molly-Mandy and little-friend-Susan set out with big baskets (to hold the blackberries) and hooked sticks (to pull the brambles nearer) and stout boots (to keep the prickles off) and old frocks (lest the thorns should catch). And they walked and they walked, till they came to a place where they knew there was always a lot of blackberries – at the proper time of year, of course.

But when they came to the place – oh, dear! – they saw a notice-board stuck up just inside

Milly-Molly-Mandy and little-friend-Susan set out

a gap in the fence. And the notice-board said, as plain as anything:

TRESPASSERS
WILL BE
PROSECUTED

Milly-Molly-Mandy and little-friend-Susan knew that meant 'You mustn't come here, because the owner doesn't want you and it's his land.'

Milly-Molly-Mandy and little-friend-Susan looked at each other very solemnly indeed. Then Milly-Molly-Mandy said, "I don't s'pose anyone would see if we went in."

And little-friend-Susan said, "I don't s'pose they'd miss any of the blackberries."

And Milly-Molly-Mandy said, "But it wouldn't be right."

And little-friend-Susan shook her head very firmly.

So they took up their baskets and sticks and moved away, trying not to feel hurt about it, although they had come a long way to that place.

They didn't know quite what to do with themselves after that, for there seemed to be no blackberries anywhere else, so they amused themselves by walking in a dry ditch close by the fence, shuffling along in the leaves with their stout little boots that were to have kept the prickles off.

And suddenly – what do you think they saw? A little ball of brown fur, just ahead of them among the grasses in the ditch.

"Is it a rabbit?" whispered little-friend-Susan. They crept closer.

"It is a rabbit!" whispered Milly-Molly-Mandy.

"Why doesn't it run away?" said little-friend-Susan, and she stroked it. The little ball of fur wriggled. Then Milly-Molly-Mandy stroked it, and it wriggled again.

Then Milly-Molly-Mandy exclaimed, "I believe it's got its head stuck in a hole in the bank!"

And they looked, and that was just what had

happened. Some earth had fallen down as bunny was burrowing, and it couldn't get its head out again.

So Milly-Molly-Mandy and little-friend-Susan carefully dug with their fingers, and loosened the earth round about, and as soon as bunny's head was free he shook his ears and stared at them.

Milly-Molly-Mandy and little-friend-Susan sat very still, and only smiled and nodded gently to show him he needn't be afraid, because they loved him.

And then little bunny turned his head and ran skitter-scutter along the ditch and up the bank, into the wood and was gone.

"Oh!" said Milly-Molly-Mandy, "we always wanted a rabbit, and now we've got one, Susan!"

"Only we'd rather ours played in the fields with his brothers and sisters instead of stopping in a poky hutch," said little-friend-Susan.

"And if we'd gone trespassing we should never have come here and found him," said Milly-Molly-Mandy. "I'd much rather have a little rabbit than a whole lot of blackberries."

And when they got back to the nice white cottage with the thatched roof, where Milly-Molly-Mandy lived, Father and Mother and Grandpa and Grandma and Uncle and Aunty all said they would much rather have a little rabbit running about in the woods than all the finest blackberries in the world.

However, the next Saturday Milly-Molly-Mandy and little-friend-Susan came upon a splendid place for blackberrying, without any notice-board; and Milly-Molly-Mandy gathered such a big basketful that there was enough to make blackberry puddings and jam and tarts and jelly and stewed blackberry-and-apple and fresh blackberries for Father and Mother and Grandpa and Grandma and Uncle and Aunty – and Milly-Molly-Mandy too.

And all the time a little rabbit skipped about in woods and thought what a lovely world it was. (And that's a true story!)

5

MILLY-MOLLY-MANDY
GOES TO A PARTY

ONCE UPON A TIME something very nice happened in the village where Milly-Molly-Mandy and her Father and Mother and Grandpa and Grandma and Uncle and Aunty lived. Some ladies clubbed together to give a party to all the children in the village, and of course Milly-Molly-Mandy was invited.

Little-friend-Susan had an invitation too, and Billy Blunt (whose father kept the corn-shop where Milly-Molly-Mandy's Uncle got his chicken feed), and Jilly, the little niece of Miss Muggins (who kept the shop where Milly-Molly-Mandy's Grandma bought her knitting-wool), and lots of others whom Milly-Molly-Mandy knew.

It was exciting.

Milly-Molly-Mandy had not been to a real party for a long time, so she was very pleased and interested when Mother said, "Well, Milly-Molly-Mandy, you must have a proper new dress for a party like this. We must think what we can do."

So Mother and Grandma and Aunty thought together for a bit, and then Mother went to the big wardrobe and rummaged in her bottom drawer until she found a most beautiful white silk scarf, which she had worn when she was married to Father, and it was just wide enough to be made into a party frock for Milly-Molly-Mandy.

Then Grandma brought out of her best handkerchief box a most beautiful lace handkerchief, which would just cut into a little collar for the neck of the party frock.

And Aunty brought out of her small top drawer some most beautiful pink ribbon, all smelling of lavender – just enough to make into a sash for the party frock.

And then Mother and Aunty set to work to cut and stitch at the party frock, while Milly-Molly-Mandy jumped up and down and handed pins when they were wanted.

The next day Father came in with a paper parcel for Milly-Molly-Mandy bulging in his coat pocket, and when Milly-Molly-Mandy unwrapped it she found the most beautiful little pair of red shoes inside!

And then Grandpa came in and held out his closed hand to Milly-Molly-Mandy, and when Milly-Molly-Mandy got his fingers open she found the most beautiful little coral necklace inside!

And then Uncle came in, and he said to Milly-Molly-Mandy, "What have I done with my handkerchief?" And he felt in all his pockets. "Oh, here it is!" And he pulled out the most beautiful little handkerchief with a pink border, which of course Milly-Molly-Mandy just knew was meant for her, and she wouldn't let Uncle wipe his nose on it, which he pretended he was going to do!

Milly-Molly-Mandy was so pleased she hugged everybody in turn – Father, Mother, Grandpa, Grandma, Uncle and Aunty.

At last the great day arrived, and little-friend-Susan, in her best spotted dress and silver bangle, called for Milly-Molly-Mandy, and they went together to the village institute, where the party was to be.

There was a lady outside who welcomed them in, and there were more ladies inside who helped them to take their things off. And everywhere looked so pretty, with garlands of coloured paper looped from the ceiling, and everybody in their best clothes.

Most of the boys and girls were looking at a row of toys on the mantelpiece, and a lady explained that they were all prizes, to be won by the children who got the most marks in the games they were going to have. There was a lovely fairy doll and a big teddy bear and a picture-book and all sorts of things.

And at the end of the row was a funny little white cotton-wool rabbit with a pointed paper hat on his head. And directly Milly-Molly-Mandy saw him she wanted him dreadfully badly, more than any of the other things.

Little-friend-Susan wanted the picture-book, and Miss Muggins' niece, Jilly, wanted the fairy doll. But the black, beady eyes of the little cotton-wool rabbit gazed so wistfully at Milly-Molly-Mandy that she determined to try ever so hard in all the games and see if she could win him.

Then the games began, and they were fun! They had a spoon-and-potato race, and musical chairs, and putting the tail on the donkey blindfold, and all sorts of guessing games.

And then they had supper – bread-and-butter with coloured hundreds-and-thousands sprinkled on, and red jellies and yellow jellies, and cakes with icing and cakes with cherries, and lemonade in red glasses.

It was quite a proper party.

And at the end the names of prize-winners were called out, and the children had to go up and receive their prizes.

At last the great day arrived

And what do you think Milly-Molly-Mandy got?

Why, she had tried so hard to win the little cotton-wool rabbit that she won first prize instead, and got the lovely fairy doll! And Miss Muggins' niece Jilly, who hadn't won any of the games, got the little cotton-wool rabbit with the sad, beady eyes – for do you know, the cotton-wool rabbit was only the booby prize, after all!

It was a lovely fairy doll, but Milly-Molly-Mandy was sure Miss Muggins' Jilly wasn't loving the booby rabbit as it ought to be loved, for its beady eyes did look so sad, and when she got near Miss Muggins' Jilly she stroked the booby rabbit, and Miss Muggins' Jilly stroked the fairy doll's hair.

Then Milly-Molly-Mandy said, "Do you love the fairy doll more than the booby rabbit?"

And Miss Muggins' Jilly said, "I should think so!"

So Milly-Molly-Mandy ran up to the lady who had given the prizes, and asked if she and Miss Muggins' Jilly might exchange prizes, and the lady said, "Yes, of course."

So Milly-Molly-Mandy and the booby rabbit went home together to the nice white cottage with the thatched roof, and Father and Mother and Grandpa and Grandma and Uncle and Aunty all liked the booby rabbit very much indeed.

And do you know, one day one of his little bead eyes dropped off, and when Mother had stuck it on again with a dab of glue, his eyes didn't look a bit sad any more, but almost as happy as Milly-Molly-Mandy's own!

6

MILLY-MOLLY-MANDY
ENJOYS A VISIT

ONCE UPON A TIME Milly-Molly-Mandy
was invited to go for a little visit to an old
friend of Mother's who lived in a nearby town.
Uncle was to take her in the pony-trap on
Saturday morning on his way to market, and
fetch her on Sunday evening, so that she
should be ready for school next day. So Milly-
Molly-Mandy would spend a whole night
away from home, which was very exciting to
think of. But just a day or two before she was
to go, Mother received a letter from her friend
to say she was so sorry, but she couldn't have
Milly-Molly-Mandy after all, as a married son
and his wife had come unexpectedly to pay her
a visit.

Milly-Molly-Mandy had to try very hard not
to feel dreadfully disappointed, for she had

never been away from home by herself before, and she had been looking forward to it so much.

"Never mind, Milly-Molly-Mandy," said Mother, when Saturday morning arrived and Milly-Molly-Mandy came down to breakfast looking rather solemn, "there are nice things happening all the time, if you keep your eyes open to see them."

Milly-Molly-Mandy said, "Yes, Muvver," in a small voice, as she took her seat, though it didn't seem just then as if anything could possibly happen as nice as going away to stay.

But while Father and Mother and Grandpa and Grandma and Uncle and Aunty and Milly-Molly-Mandy were at breakfast Mrs Moggs, who was little-friend-Susan's mother, came round in a great hurry without a hat. And Mrs Moggs told them how some friends who had to go to the town on business, had offered her a seat in their gig. And as Mrs Moggs' mother lived there Mrs Moggs thought it was a nice opportunity to go and see her, only she didn't like leaving Susan alone all day, Mr Moggs being out at work.

So Milly-Molly-Mandy's mother said, "Let her come round here, Mrs Moggs. Milly-Molly-Mandy would like to have her. And I don't suppose you'll be back till late, so she'd better spend the night here too."

Milly-Molly-Mandy was pleased, and Mrs Moggs thanked them very much indeed, and they all wished Mrs Moggs a nice trip, and then Mrs Moggs ran back home to get ready.

"Where will Susan sleep? In the spare room?" asked Milly-Molly-Mandy, making haste to finish her breakfast.

"Yes," said Mother, "and you had better sleep there too, to keep her company."

Milly-Molly-Mandy was very much pleased at that, for she had never slept in the spare room – her cot-bed was in one corner of Father's and Mother's room.

"Why, Muvver!" she said. "I can't have a visit of my own, but I'll just be able to enjoy Susan's instead, shan't I? P'r'aps it'll be almost quite as nice!"

She helped to wash up the breakfast things, and to make the spare room bed, and to dust.

And then she was just looking out of the

window, thinking how nice it would be for Susan to wake up in the morning with a new view outside, when what did she see but little-friend-Susan herself, trudging along up the road with a basket on one arm and her coat on the other. So she ran down to the gate to welcome her in.

And though Milly-Molly-Mandy and little-friend-Susan met almost every day, and very often spent the whole day together, somehow it felt so different to think little-friend-Susan was going to stay the night with Milly-Molly-Mandy that they couldn't help giving an extra skip or two after they had kissed each other.

Milly-Molly-Mandy took her to see Mother, and then they went up to the spare room to unpack little-friend-Susan's basket.

They put her nightgown and brush and comb and toothbrush and slippers in their proper places, and decided which sides of the bed they were going to sleep – and they found each wanted the side that the other one didn't, which was nice – though of course Milly-Molly-Mandy would have given little-friend-Susan first choice, anyway.

Then Milly-Molly-Mandy showed little-friend-Susan round the room, and let her admire the fat silk pin-cushion on the dressing-table, and the hair-tidy that Aunty had paint-ed, and the ornaments on the chest of drawers – the china dogs with the rough-feeling coats, and the little girl with the china lace skirt.

And while they were looking at the fretwork bracket which Father had made for Mother before they were married, Aunty came running up to say Uncle was just going to drive to mar-ket, and they might go with him if they were quick.

So they scrambled into their coats and hats, and Milly-Molly-Mandy ran to ask Mother in

a whisper if she might take a penny from her money box to spend in town. And soon they were sitting up close together beside Uncle in the high pony-trap, while the little brown pony (whose name was Twinkletoes) trotted briskly along the white road.

Little-friend-Susan hadn't been for many drives. Milly-Molly-Mandy often went, but she enjoyed this one much more than usual, because little-friend-Susan was so interested and pleased with everything.

Billy Blunt was whipping a top outside his father's corn-shop as they drove through the village. They waved to him, and he waved back. And a little farther on Miss Muggins' niece, Jilly, was wheeling her doll's pram along the pavement, and called out, "Hello, Milly-Molly-Mandy! Hello, Susan!"

And then they drove along a road through corn fields, where the little green blades of wheat were busy growing up to make big loaves of bread – which is why you must never interrupt them by walking in the corn, even if you see a poppy.

When they came to the town there were

crowds of people everywhere, shouting about the things they had to sell. And Milly-Molly-Mandy and little-friend-Susan followed Uncle about the market-place, looking at all the stalls of fruit and sweets and books and fish and clothes and a hundred other things.

Milly-Molly-Mandy spent her penny on a big yellow sugar-stick for little-friend-Susan, who broke it carefully in two, and gave her half.

When Uncle had done his business he took them to have dinner at a place where all the tables had marble tops, which made such a sharp clatter unless you put your glass down very gently. There were crowds of people eating at other tables round about, and a lot of talking and clattering of cups and plates. It was very exciting. Little-friend-Susan was having a splendid holiday.

When they had finished Uncle paid the bill and led the way back to where Twinkletoes was waiting patiently, munching in his nose-bag. And off they drove again, clippety-cloppety, with Uncle's parcels stowed under the seat.

Unpacking little-friend-Susan's basket

And when they got near home it did seem queer for Milly-Molly-Mandy and little-friend-Susan to go straight past the Moggs' cottage and not have to stop and say goodbye to each other. They squeezed each other's hand all the rest of the way home to the nice white cottage with the thatched roof, because they felt so pleased.

When bedtime drew near they had their baths together, just as if they were sisters. And then Milly-Molly-Mandy in her red dressing-gown, and little-friend-Susan in Grandma's red shawl, sat in front of the fire on little stools (with Toby the dog on one side, and Topsy the cat on the other), while Mother made them each a lid-potato for their suppers.

First Mother took two well-baked potatoes out of the oven. Then she nearly cut the tops off them – but not quite. Then she scooped all the potato out of the skins and mashed it up with a little salt and a little pepper and a lot of butter. And then she pushed it back into the two potato-skins, and shut the tops like little lids.

Then Milly-Molly-Mandy and little-friend-

Susan were given a mug of milk and a plate of bread-and-butter, and one of the nice warm lid-potatoes. And they opened the potato-lids and ate out of them with little spoons.

They did enjoy their suppers.

And when the last bit was gone Mother said, "Now, you two, I've set the candle in your room, and I'll be up to fetch it in ten minutes."

So Milly-Molly-Mandy and little-friend-Susan kissed goodnight to Father and Mother and Grandpa and Grandma and Uncle and Aunty, and stroked Toby the dog and Topsy the cat. And then they went upstairs to bed, hopping and skipping all the way, because they were so pleased they were going to sleep together in the spare room.

And next day, when Mrs Moggs came round to tell how she had enjoyed her trip, and to fetch Susan, Milly-Molly-Mandy said, "Thank you very much indeed, Mrs Moggs, for Susan's visit. I have enjoyed it!"

7
MILLY-MOLLY-MANDY
GOES GARDENING

ONCE UPON A TIME, one Saturday morning, Milly-Molly-Mandy went down to the village. She had to go to Mr Blunt's corn-shop to order a list of things for Uncle – and would Mr Blunt please send them on Monday without fail?

Mr Blunt said, "Surely, surely! Tell your uncle he shall have them first thing in the morning."

And then Milly-Molly-Mandy, who loved the smell of the corn-shop, peeped into the great bins, and dug her hands down into the maize and bran and oats and let them sift through her fingers. And then she said good-bye and came out.

As she passed the Blunts' little garden at the side of the shop she saw Billy Blunt's back, bending down just the other side of the palings. It looked very busy.

Billy Blunt was a little bigger than Milly-Molly-Mandy, and she did not know him very well, but they always said "Hullo!" when they met.

So Milly-Molly-Mandy peeped through the palings and said, "Hullo, Billy!"

Billly Blunt looked round for a moment and said, "Hullo!" And then he turned back to his work.

But he didn't say, "Hullo, Milly-Molly-Mandy!" and he didn't smile. So Milly-Molly-Mandy stuck her toes in the fence and hung on and looked over the top.

"What's the matter?" Milly-Molly-Mandy asked.

Billy Blunt looked round again. "Nothing's the matter," he said gloomily. "Only I've got to weed these old flower-beds right up to the house."

"I don't mind weeding," said Milly-Molly-Mandy.

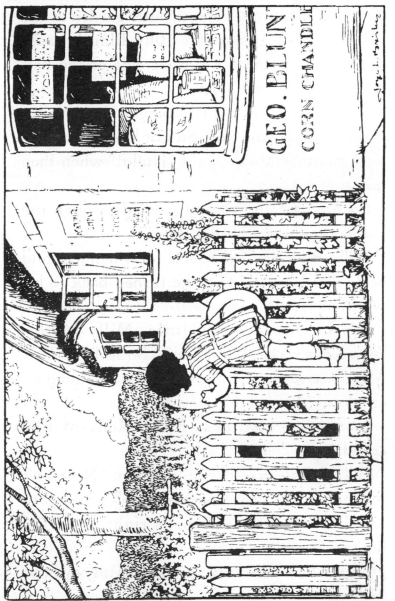

"What's the matter?" Milly-Molly-Mandy asked

"Huh! You try it here, and see how you like it!" said Billy Blunt. "The earth's as hard as nails, and the weeds have got roots pretty near a mile long."

Milly-Molly-Mandy wasn't quite sure whether he meant it as an invitation, but anyhow she accepted it as one, and pushed open the little white gate and came into the Blunts' garden.

It was a nice garden, smelling of wallflowers.

Billy Blunt said, "There's a garden-fork." So Milly-Molly-Mandy took it up and started work on the other side of the flower-bed which bordered the little brick path up to the house. And they dug away together.

Presently Milly-Molly-Mandy said, "Doesn't the earth smell nice when you turn it up?"

And Billy Blunt said, "Does it? Yes, it does rather." And they went on weeding.

Presently Milly-Molly-Mandy, pulling tufts of grass out of the pansies, asked, "What do you do this for, if you don't like it?"

And Billy Blunt, tugging at a dandelion root, grunted and said, "Father says I ought to be making myself useful."

60

"That's our sort of fruit," said Milly-Molly-Mandy.

"My Muvver says we'd be like apple-trees which didn't grow apples if we didn't be useful."

"Huh!" said Billy Blunt. "Funny idea, us growing fruit! Never thought of it like that." And they went on weeding.

Presently Milly-Molly-Mandy asked, "Why're there all those little holes in the lawn?"

"Dad's been digging out dandelions," said Billy Blunt. "He wants to make the garden nice."

Then Milly-Molly-Mandy said, "There's lots of grass here, only it oughtn't to be. We might plant it in the holes."

"Umm!" said Billy Blunt, "and then we'll be making the lawn look as tidy as the beds. Let's!"

So they dug, and they turned the earth, and they pulled out what didn't belong there. And all the weeds they threw into a heap to be burned, and all the tufts of grass they carefully planted in the lawn. And after a time the flower-beds began to look most beautifully neat, and you could see hardly any bald places on the lawn.

Presently Mr Blunt came out of the shop on to the pavement. He had a can of green paint and a brush in his hand, and he reached over the palings and set them down among the daisies on the lawn.

"Hullo, Milly-Molly-Mandy!" said Mr Blunt. "Thought you'd gone home. Well, you two have been doing good work on those beds there. Billy, I'm going to paint the water-butt and the handle of the roller some time. Perhaps you'd like to do it for me? You'll have to clean off the rust first with sand-paper."

Billy Blunt and Milly-Molly-Mandy looked quite eager.

Billy Blunt said, "Rather, Dad!" And Milly-Molly-Mandy looked with great interest at the green can and the garden-roller. But she knew she ought to be starting back to dinner at the nice white cottage with the thatched roof, or Father and Mother and Grandpa and Grandma and Uncle and Aunty would be wondering what had become of her. So she handed her garden fork back to Billy Blunt and walked slowly to the gate.

But Billy Blunt said, "Couldn't you come again after dinner? I'll save you some of the painting."

So Milly-Molly-Mandy gave a little skip and said, "I'd like to, if Muvver doesn't want me."

So after dinner, when she had helped with the washing-up, Milly-Molly-Mandy ran hoppity-skip all the way down to the village again. And there in the Blunts' garden was Billy Blunt, busy rubbing the iron bands on the water-butt with a sheet of sand-paper.

"Hullo, Billy!" said Milly-Molly-Mandy.

"Hullo, Milly-Molly-Mandy!" said Billy Blunt.

He looked very hot and dirty, but he smiled

quite broadly. And then he said, "I've saved the garden-roller for you to paint – it's all sand-papered ready."

Milly-Molly-Mandy thought that was nice of Billy Blunt, for the sand-papering was the nasty, dirty part of the work.

Billy Blunt got the lid off the can, and stirred up the beautiful green paint with a stick. Then all by himself he thought of fetching a piece of newspaper to pin over her frock to keep her clean. And then he went back to rubbing the water-butt, while Milly-Molly-Mandy dipped the brush carefully into the lovely full can of green paint, and started work on the lawn mower.

The handle had a pattern in wriggly bits of iron, and it was great fun getting the paint into all the cracks. And you can't imagine how beautiful and new that roller looked when the paint was on it.

Billy Blunt had to keep leaving his water-butt to see how it was going on, because the wriggly bits looked so nice when they were green, and he hadn't any wriggly bits on his water-butt.

By the end of the afternoon you ought to have seen how nice the garden looked! The flower-beds were clean and trim, the lawn tidied up, the water-butt stood glistening green by the side of the house, and the roller lay glistening green on the grass.

And when Mr Blunt came out and saw it all he was pleased!

He called Mrs Blunt, and Mrs Blunt was pleased too. She gave them each a banana, and they ate them sitting on one of the corn-bins in the shop.

And afterwards Billy Blunt buried Milly-Molly-Mandy in the corn, right up to the neck. And when he helped her out again she was all bits of corn, down her neck, and in her socks, and on her hair. But Milly-Molly-Mandy didn't mind a scrap. She liked it.

8

MILLY-MOLLY-MANDY
KEEPS SHOP

ONCE UPON A TIME Milly-Molly-Mandy was walking home from school with some little friends – Billy Blunt, Miss Muggins' niece Jilly, and, of course, little-friend-Susan. And they were all talking about what they would like to do when they were big.

Billy Blunt said he would have a motor-bus and drive people to the station and pull their boxes about. Miss Muggins' Jilly said she would curl her hair and be a lady who acts for the pictures. Little-friend-Susan wanted to be a nurse with long white streamers, and push a pram with two babies in it.

Milly-Molly-Mandy wanted a shop like Miss Muggins', where she could sell sweets, and cut pretty coloured stuff for people's dresses with a big pair of scissors. And, "Oh, dear!" said Milly-Molly-Mandy, "I wish we didn't have to wait till we had growed up!"

Then they came to Miss Muggins' shop, and Jilly said "Goodbye," and went in.

And then they came to Mr Blunt's corn-shop which was only a few steps farther on, and Billy Blunt said "Goodbye," and went in.

And then Milly-Molly-Mandy and little-friend-Susan, with their arms round each other, walked up the white road with the fields each side till they came to the Moggs' cottage, and little-friend-Susan said, "Goodbye" and went in.

And Milly-Molly-Mandy went hoppity-skipping on alone till she came to the nice white

cottage with the thatched roof, where Mother
was at the gate to meet her.

Next day was Saturday, and Milly-Molly-
Mandy went down to the village on an errand
for Mother. And when she had done it she saw
Miss Muggins standing at her shop door, looking rather worried.

And when Miss Muggins saw Milly-Molly-
Mandy she said, "Oh, Milly-Molly-Mandy,
would you mind running to ask Mrs Jakes if
she could come and mind my shop for an
hour? Tell her I've got to go to see someone on
very important business, and I don't know
what to do, and Jilly's gone picnicking."

So Milly-Molly-Mandy ran to ask Mrs
Jakes. But Mrs Jakes said, "Tell Miss
Muggins I'm very sorry, but I've just got the
cakes in the oven, and I can't leave them."

So Milly-Molly-Mandy ran back and told
Miss Muggins, and Miss Muggins said, "I
wonder if Mrs Blunt would come."

So Milly-Molly-Mandy ran to ask Mrs
Blunt. But Mrs Blunt said, "I'm sorry, but I'm
simply up to my eyes in house-cleaning, and I
can't leave just now."

So Milly-Molly-Mandy ran back and told Miss Muggins, and Miss Muggins said she didn't know of anyone else she could ask.

Then Milly-Molly-Mandy said, "Oh, Miss Muggins, couldn't I look after the shop for you? I'll tell people you'll be back in an hour, and if they only want a sugar-stick or something I could give it them – I know how much it is!"

Miss Muggins looked at Milly-Molly-Mandy, and then she said: "Well, you aren't very big, but I know you're careful, Milly-Molly-Mandy."

So she gave her lots of instructions about asking people if they would come back in an hour, and not selling things unless she was quite sure of the price, and so on. And then Miss Muggins put on her hat and feather boa and hurried off.

And Milly-Molly-Mandy was left alone in charge of the shop!

Milly-Molly-Mandy felt very solemn and careful indeed. She dusted the counter with a duster which she saw hanging on a nail; and then she peeped into the window at all the handkerchiefs and socks and bottles of sweets – and she could see Mrs Hubble arranging the loaves and cakes in her shop window opposite, and Mr Smale (who had the grocer's shop with a little counter at the back where you posted parcels and bought stamps and letter-paper) standing at his door enjoying the sunshine. And Milly-Molly-Mandy felt so pleased that she had a shop as well as they.

And then, suddenly, the door-handle rattled, and the little bell over the door jangle-jangled up and down, and who should come in but little-friend-Susan! And how little-friend-Susan did stare when she saw Milly-Molly-Mandy behind the counter!

"Miss Muggins has gone out on 'portant business, but she'll be back in an hour. What do you want?" said Milly-Molly-Mandy.

"A packet of safety-pins for Mother. What are you doing here?" said little-friend-Susan.

"I'm looking after the shop," said Milly-Molly-Mandy. "And I know where the safety-pins are, because I had to buy some yester-day."

So Milly-Molly-Mandy wrapped up the

safety-pins in a piece of thin brown paper, and twisted the end just as Miss Muggins did. And she handed the packet to little-friend-Susan, and little-friend-Susan handed her a penny.

And then little-friend-Susan wanted to stay and play 'shops' with Milly-Molly-Mandy.

But Milly-Molly-Mandy shook her head solemnly and said, "No, this isn't play: it's business. I've got to be very, very careful. You'd better go, Susan."

And just then the bell jangled again, and a lady came in, so little-friend-Susan went out. (She peered through the window for a time to see how Milly-Molly-Mandy got on, but Milly-Molly-Mandy wouldn't look at her.)

The lady was Miss Bloss, who lived opposite, over the baker's shop, with Mrs Bloss. She wanted a quarter of a yard of pink flannelette, because she was making a wrapper for her mother, and she hadn't bought quite enough for the collar. She said she didn't like to waste a whole hour till Miss Muggins returned.

Milly-Molly-Mandy stood on one leg and wondered what to do, and Miss Bloss tapped with one finger and wondered what to do.

And then Miss Bloss said, "That's the roll my flannelette came off. I'm quite sure Miss Muggins wouldn't mind my taking some."

So between them they measured off the pink flannelette, and Milly-Molly-Mandy fetched Miss Muggins' big scissors, and Miss Bloss made a crease exactly where the quarter-yard came; and Milly-Molly-Mandy breathed very hard and cut slowly and carefully right along the crease to the end.

And then she wrapped the piece up and gave it to Miss Bloss, and Miss Bloss handed her half a crown, saying, "Ask Miss Muggins to send me the change when she gets back."

And then Miss Bloss went out.

And then for a time nobody came in, and Milly-Molly-Mandy amused herself by trying to find the rolls of stuff that different people's dresses had come off. There was her own pink-and-white-striped cotton (looking so lovely and new) and Mother's blue checked apron stuff and Mrs Jakes' Sunday gown . . .

Then rattle went the handle and jangle went the bell, and who should come in but Billy Blunt!

"I'm Miss Muggins," said Milly-Molly-Mandy. "What do you want to buy?"

"Where's Miss Muggins?" said Billy Blunt.

So Milly-Molly-Mandy had to explain again. And then Billy Blunt said he had wanted a penny-worth of aniseed balls. So Milly-Molly-Mandy stood on a box and reached down the glass jar from the shelf.

They were twelve a penny she knew, for she had often bought them. So she counted them out, and then Billy Blunt counted them.

And Billy Blunt said, "You've got one too many here."

So Milly-Molly-Mandy counted again, and she found one too many too. So they dropped one back in the jar, and Milly-Molly-Mandy put the others into a little bag and swung it over by the corners, just as Miss Muggins did, and gave it to Billy Blunt. And Billy Blunt gave her his penny.

And then Billy Blunt grinned, and said, "Good morning, ma'am"

"I'm Miss Muggins. What do you want to buy?"

And Milly-Molly-Mandy said, "Good morning, sir," and Billy Blunt went out.

After that an hour began to seem rather a long time, with the sun shining so outside. But at last the little bell gave a lively jangle again, and Miss Muggins had returned!

And though Milly-Molly-Mandy had enjoyed herself very much, she thought perhaps, after all, she would rather wait until she was grown up before she kept a shop for herself.

9

MILLY-MOLLY-MANDY

GIVES A PARTY

ONCE UPON A TIME Milly-Molly-Mandy had a plan. And when she had thought over the plan for a while she went to look in her money-box. And in the money-box were four pennies and a ha'penny, which Milly-Molly-Mandy did not think would be enough for her plan. So Milly-Molly-Mandy went off to talk it over with little-friend-Susan down the road.

"Susan," said Milly-Molly-Mandy, "I've got a plan (only it's a great secret). I want to give a party in our barn to Farver and Muvver and Grandpa and Grandma and Uncle and Aunty. And I want to buy refreshments. And you and I will be waitresses. And if there's anything over we can eat it up afterwards."

Little-friend-Susan thought it a very good plan indeed.

"Will we wear caps?" she asked.

"Yes," said Milly-Molly-Mandy, "and aprons. Only I haven't got enough money for the refreshments, so I don't think there'll be any over. We must think."

So Milly-Molly-Mandy and little-friend-Susan sat down and thought hard.

"We must work and earn some," said Milly-Molly-Mandy.

"But how?" said little-friend-Susan.

"We might sell something," said Milly-Molly-Mandy.

"But what?" said little-friend-Susan. So they had to think some more.

Presently Milly-Molly-Mandy said, "I've got pansies and marigolds in my garden."

And little-friend-Susan said, "I've got nasturtiums in mine."

"We could run errands for people," said Milly-Molly-Mandy.

"And clean brass," said little-friend-Susan.

That was a lovely idea, so Milly-Molly-Mandy fetched a pencil and paper and wrote out very carefully:

> *Millicent Margaret Amanda & Susan &*
> *Co. have bunches of flowers for sale and*
> *clean brass very cheap (we do not spill the*
> *polish) and run errands very cheap.*

"What's 'and Co.'?" said little-friend-Susan.

"It's just business," said Milly-Molly-Mandy, "but perhaps we might ask Billy Blunt to be it. And he could be a waiter."

Then they hung the notice on the front gate, and waited just the other side of the hedge.

Several people passed, but nobody seemed to want anything. Then at last a motor-car came along with a lady and gentleman in it; and when they saw the nice white cottage with the thatched roof they stopped at the gate to ask if they could get some cream there.

Milly-Molly-Mandy said, "I'll go and ask Muvver," and took the little pot they held out. And when she came back with it full of cream the lady and gentleman had read the notice and were asking little-friend-Susan questions. As the lady paid for the cream she said they must certainly have some flowers. So they each bought a bunch. And then the gentleman said the round brass thing in front of his car needed cleaning very badly – could the firm do it straight away?

So Milly-Molly-Mandy said, "Yes, sir," and raced back to the cottage to give Mother the cream-money and to borrow the brass-polishing box. And then she cleaned the round brass thing in front of the car with one piece of cloth and little-friend-Susan rubbed it bright with another piece of cloth, and the lady and gentleman looked on and seemed very satisfied.

Then the gentleman asked, "How much?" and paid them two pence for the flowers and a penny for the polishing. Milly-Molly-Mandy wanted to do some more polishing for the money, but the gentleman said they couldn't stop. And then they said goodbye and went off, and the lady turned and waved, and Milly-Molly-Mandy and little-friend-Susan waved back until they were gone.

Milly-Molly-Mandy and little-friend-Susan felt very happy and pleased.

And now they had sevenpence-ha'penny for the refreshments. Father and Mother and Grandpa and Grandma and Uncle and Aunty and Mrs Moggs, little-friend-Susan's mother, made seven.

Then who should look over the hedge but Mr Jakes, the Postman, on his way home from collecting letters from the letter-boxes. He had seen the notice on the gate.

"What's this? You trying to make a fortune?" said the Postman.

"Yes," said Milly-Molly-Mandy, "we've earned three pence!"

"My! And what do you plan to do with it?" said the Postman.

"We've got a secret!" said Milly-Molly-Mandy, with a little skip.

"Ah!" said the Postman, "I guess it's a nice one, too!"

"Milly-Molly-Mandy looked at little-friend-Susan, and then she looked at the Postman. He was a nice Postman. "You won't tell if we tell you?" she asked.

"Try me!" said the Postman promptly. So Milly-Molly-Mandy told him they were planning to give a party to Father and Mother and Grandpa and Grandma and Uncle and Aunty and Mrs Moggs.

"They're in luck, they are!" said the Postman. "Nobody asks me to parties."

Milly-Molly-Mandy looked at little-friend-Susan again, and then she looked at the Postman. He was a very nice Postman. Then she said, "Supposing you were invited, would you come?"

"You try me!" said the Postman promptly again. And then he hitched up his letter-bag and went on.

"Farver and Muvver and Grandpa and Grandma and Uncle and Aunty and Mrs Moggs and the Postman. We've got to earn some more," said Milly-Molly-Mandy. "Let's go down to the village and ask Billy Blunt to be 'and Co.,' and p'r'aps he'll have an idea."

Billy Blunt was in the road outside the corn-shop, mending the handles of his box on wheels. He had made it nearly all himself, and it was a very nice one, painted green like the water-butt and the lawn roller. He thought 'and Co.' was rather a funny name, but he said he would be it all right, and offered to make them a box with a slit in it, where they could keep their earnings. And he put in four

81

farthings out of his collection. (Billy Blunt was collecting farthings – he had nineteen in an empty bird seed bag.)

So now they had eightpence-ha'penny for the refreshments.

On Monday morning, on their way home to dinner, Milly-Molly-Mandy and little-friend-Susan passed Mrs Jakes, the Postman's wife, at her door, getting a breath of fresh air before dishing up her dinner. And Mrs Jakes said, "Good morning! How's the firm of Millicent Margaret Amanda, Susan, and Co. getting on?"

Milly-Molly-Mandy said, "Very well, thank you!"

"My husband's told me about your brass-cleaning," said Mrs Jakes. "I've got a whole mantel-shelf full that wants doing!"

Milly-Molly-Mandy and little-friend-Susan were very pleased, and arranged to come in directly school was over in the afternoon and clean it.

And they cleaned a mug and three candle-sticks and two lamps – one big and one little – and a tray and a warming-pan, and they didn't spill or waste any of the polish. Mrs Jakes seemed very satisfied, and gave them each a penny and a piece of cake.

So now they had tenpence-ha'penny for refreshments.

But when they got outside Milly-Molly-Mandy said, "Farver and Muvver and Grandpa and Grandma and Uncle and Aunty and Mrs Moggs and the Postman and Mrs Postman – I wonder if we've earned enough, Susan!"

As they turned home they passed the forge, and of course they had to stop a moment at the doorway, as usual, to watch the fire roaring, and Mr Rudge the Blacksmith banging with his hammer on the anvil.

Little-friend-Susan was just a bit nervous of

the Blacksmith – he was so big, and his face was so dirty it made his teeth look very white and his eyes very twinkly when he smiled at them. But Milly-Molly-Mandy knew he was nice and clean under the dirt, which he couldn't help while he worked. So she smiled back.

And the Blacksmith said, "Hullo!"

And Milly-Molly-Mandy said, "Hullo!"

Then the Blacksmith beckoned with his finger and said, "Come here!"

Milly-Molly-Mandy gave a little jump, and little-friend-Susan pulled at her hand, but Milly-Molly-Mandy knew he was really just a nice man under the dirt, so she went up to him.

And the Blacksmith said, "Look what I've got here!" And he showed them a tiny little horseshoe, just like a proper one, only smaller, which he had made for them to keep. Milly-Molly-Mandy and little-friend-Susan were pleased!

Milly-Molly-Mandy thanked him very much. And then she looked at the Blacksmith and said, "If you were invited to a party, would you come?"

And the Blacksmith looked at Milly-Molly-Mandy with twinkly eyes and said he'd come quite fast – so long as it wasn't before five o'clock on Saturday, when he was playing cricket with his team in the meadow.

When they got outside again Milly-Molly-Mandy said, "Farver and Muvver and Grandpa and Grandma and Uncle and Aunty and Mrs Moggs and the Postman and Mrs Postman and the Blacksmith. We'll ask them for half-past five, and we ought to earn some more money, Susan!"

Just then they met Billy Blunt coming along, pulling his box on wheels with a bundle in it. And Billy Blunt grinned and said, "I'm fetching Mrs Bloss's washing, for the firm!" Milly-Molly-Mandy and little-friend-Susan were pleased!

When Saturday morning came all the invitations had been given out, and the firm of Millicent Margaret Amanda, Susan and Co. was very busy putting things tidy in the barn, and covering up things which couldn't be moved with lots of green branches which Grandpa was trimming from the hedges.

And when half-past five came Milly-Molly-Mandy and little-friend-Susan, with clean hands and paper caps and aprons, waited by the barn door to welcome the guests. And each gentleman received a marigold buttonhole, and each lady a pansy.

Everybody arrived in good time, except the Blacksmith, who was just a bit late – he looked so clean and pink in his white cricket flannels, Milly-Molly-Mandy hardly knew him – and Billy Blunt. But Billy Blunt came lugging a gramophone and two records which he had borrowed from a bigger boy at school. (He never told, but he had given the boy all the rest of his collection of farthings – fifteen of them, which makes three-pence-three-farthings – in exchange.)

Then Billy Blunt, who didn't want to dance, looked after the gramophone, while Father and Mother and Grandpa and Grandma and Uncle and Aunty and Mrs Moggs and the Postman and Mrs Postman and the Blacksmith and Milly-Molly-Mandy and little-friend-Susan danced together in the old barn till the dust flew. And Milly-Molly-Mandy danced a lot

And then there were refreshments

with the Blacksmith as well as with everybody else, and so did little-friend-Susan.

They did enjoy themselves!

And then there were refreshments – raspberry drops and aniseed balls on saucers trimmed with little flowers; and late blackberries on leaf plates; and sherbet drinks, which Billy Blunt prepared while Milly-Molly-Mandy and little-friend-Susan stood by to tell people just the very moment to drink, when it was fizzing properly. (It was exciting!) And a jelly which Milly-Molly-Mandy and little-friend-Susan had made themselves from a packet, only it had to be eaten rather like soup, as it wouldn't stand up properly.

But Father and Mother and Grandpa and Grandma and Uncle and Aunty and Mrs Moggs and the Postman and Mrs Postman and the Blacksmith all said they had never enjoyed a jelly so much. And the Blacksmith, in a big voice, proposed a vote of thanks to the firm for the delightful party and refreshments, and everybody else said "Hear! Hear!" and clapped. And Milly-Molly-Mandy and little-friend-Susan joined in the clapping too, which

wasn't quite proper, but they were so happy
they couldn't help it!

And then all the guests went home.

And when the firm came to clear up the
refreshments they found there was only one
aniseed ball left. But placed among the empty
saucers and glasses on the bench were a small
basket of pears and a bag of mixed sweets with
a ticket "For the Waiter and Waitresses" on it!

10

MILLY-MOLLY-MANDY
GETS TO KNOW TEACHER

ONCE UPON A TIME there were changes at
Milly-Molly-Mandy's school. Miss Sheppard,
the head-mistress, was going away, and Miss
Edwards, the second teacher, was to be head-
mistress in her place, and live in the teacher's
cottage just by the school, instead of coming in
by the bus from the town each day.

Miss Edwards was very strict, and taught
arithmetic and history and geography, and
wore high collars.

Milly-Molly-Mandy wasn't particularly
interested in the change, though she liked both
Miss Sheppard and Miss Edwards quite well.
But one afternoon Miss Edwards gave her a
note to give to her Mother, and the note was to

ask if Milly-Molly-Mandy's Mother would be so very good as to let Miss Edwards have a bed at the nice white cottage with the thatched roof for a night or two until Miss Edwards got her new little house straight.

Father and Mother and Grandpa and Grandma and Uncle and Aunty talked it over during supper, and they thought they might manage it for a few nights.

Milly-Molly-Mandy was very interested, and tried to think what it would be like to have Teacher sitting at supper with them, and going to sleep in the spare room, as well as teaching in school all day. And she couldn't help feeling just a little bit glad that it was only to be for a night or two.

Next day she took a note to school for Teacher from Mother, to say, yes, they would be pleased to have her. And after school Milly-Molly-Mandy told little-friend-Susan and Billy Blunt about it.

And little-friend-Susan said, "Ooh! Won't you have to behave properly! I'm glad she's not coming to us!"

And Billy Blunt said, "Huh! – hard lines!"

91

Milly-Molly-Mandy was quite glad Teacher was only coming to stay for a few nights.

Miss Edwards arrived at the nice white cottage with the thatched roof just before supper time the following evening.

Milly-Molly-Mandy was looking out for her, and directly she heard the gate click she called Mother and ran and opened the front door wide, so that the hall lamp could shine down the path. And Teacher came in out of the dark, just as Mother hurried from the kitchen to welcome her.

Teacher thanked Mother very much for having her, and said she felt so dusty and untidy because she had been putting up shelves in her new little cottage ever since school was over.

So Mother said, "Come right up to your room, Miss Edwards, and Milly-Molly-Mandy will bring you a jug of hot water. And then I expect you'll be glad of some supper straight away!"

So Milly-Molly-Mandy ran along to the kitchen for a jug of hot water, thinking how funny it was to hear Teacher's familiar voice away from school. She tapped very politely at the half-open door of the spare room (she could see Teacher tidying her hair in front of the dressing-table, by the candlelight), and Teacher smiled at her as she took the steaming jug, and said:

"That's kind of you, Milly-Molly-Mandy! This is just what I want most. What a lovely smell of hot cakes!"

Milly-Molly-Mandy smiled back, though she was quite a bit surprised that Teacher should speak in that pleased, hungry sort of way – it was more the kind of way she, or little-friend-Susan, or Father or Mother or Grandpa or Grandma or Uncle or Aunty, might have spoken.

When Teacher came downstairs to the kitchen they all sat down to supper. Teacher's place was just opposite Milly-Molly-Mandy's and every time she caught Milly-Molly-Mandy's eye she smiled across at her. And Milly-Molly-Mandy smiled back, and tried to remember to sit up, for she kept on almost expecting Teacher to say, "Head up, Milly-Molly-Mandy! Keep your elbows off the desk!" – but she never did!

They were all a little shy of Teacher, just at first; but soon Father and Mother and Grandpa and Grandma and Uncle and Aunty were talking away, and Teacher was talking too, and laughing. And she looked so different when she was laughing that Milly-Molly-Mandy found it quite difficult to get on with her bread-and-milk before it got cold. Teacher enjoyed the hot cakes, and wanted to know just how Mother made them. She asked a lot of questions, and Mother said she would teach Teacher how to do it, so that she could make them in her own new little kitchen.

Milly-Molly-Mandy thought how funny it would be for Teacher to start having lessons.

After supper Teacher asked Milly-Molly-Mandy if she could make little sailor-girls, and when Milly-Molly-Mandy said no, Teacher drew a little sailor-girl, with a sailor-collar and sailor-hat and pleated skirt, on a folded piece of paper, and then she cut it out with Aunty's scissors. And when she unfolded the paper there was a whole row of little sailor-girls all holding hands.

Milly-Molly-Mandy did like it. She thought

how funny it was that she should have known Teacher all that time and never known she could draw little sailor-girls.

Then Mother said, "Now, Milly-Molly-Mandy, it is bedtime." So Milly-Molly-Mandy kissed Father and Mother and Grandpa and Grandma and Uncle and Aunty, and went to shake hands with Teacher. But Teacher said she wanted a kiss too. So they kissed each other in quite a nice friendly way.

But still Milly-Molly-Mandy felt when she went upstairs she must get into bed extra quickly and quietly, because Teacher was in the house.

Next morning Milly-Molly-Mandy and Teacher went to school together. And as soon as they got there Teacher was just her usual self again, and told Milly-Molly-Mandy to sit up, or to get on with her work, as if she had never laughed at supper, or cut out little sailor-girls, or kissed anyone goodnight.

After school Milly-Molly-Mandy showed little-friend-Susan and Billy Blunt the row of little sailor-girls.

And little-friend-Susan opened her eyes and

said, "Just fancy Teacher doing that!"

And Billy Blunt folded them up carefully in the creases so that he could see how they were made, and then he grinned and gave them back.

And little-friend-Susan and Billy Blunt didn't feel so very sorry for Milly-Molly-Mandy having Teacher to stay, then.

That evening Teacher came up to the nice white cottage with the thatched roof earlier than she did the day before. And when Milly-Molly-Mandy came into the kitchen from taking a nice meal out to Toby the dog, and giving him a good bedtime romp round the yard, what did she see but Teacher, with one of Mother's big aprons on and her sleeves tucked up, learning how to make apple turn-overs for supper! And Mother was saying, "Always mix pastry with a light hand," and Teacher was looking so interested, and didn't seem in the least to know she had a streak of flour down one cheek.

When Teacher saw Milly-Molly-Mandy she said, "Come along, Milly-Molly-Mandy, and have a cooking lesson with me, it's such fun!"

What did she see but Teacher learning how to make apple turn-overs

So Milly-Molly-Mandy's Mother gave her a little piece of dough, and she stood by Teacher's side, rolling it out and making it into a ball again; but she was much more interested in watching Teacher being taught. And Teacher did everything she was told, and tried so hard that her cheeks got quite pink.

When the turn-overs were all made there was a small piece of dough left on the board, so Teacher shaped it into the most beautiful little bird; and the bird and the turn-overs were all popped into the oven, together with Milly-Molly-Mandy's piece (which had been a pig and a cat and a teapot, but ended up a little grey loaf).

When Father and Mother and Grandpa and Grandma and Uncle and Aunty and Teacher and Milly-Molly-Mandy sat down to supper, Teacher put her finger on her lips to Milly-Molly-Mandy when the apple turn-overs came on, so that Milly-Molly-Mandy shouldn't tell who made them until they had been tasted. And Teacher watched anxiously, and presently Mother said, "How do you like these turn-overs?" And everybody said they were most delicious, and then Milly-Molly-Mandy couldn't wait any longer, and she called out, "Teacher made them!" and everybody was so surprised.

Milly-Molly-Mandy didn't eat the little grey-brown loaf, because she didn't quite fancy it (Toby the dog did, though), and she felt she couldn't eat the little golden-brown bird, because it really looked too good to be eaten just yet. So she took it to school with her next day, to share with little-friend-Susan and Billy Blunt.

And little-friend-Susan said, "Isn't it pretty? Isn't Teacher clever?"

And Billy Blunt said, "Fancy Teacher playing with dough!"

And little-friend-Susan and Billy Blunt didn't feel at all sorry for Milly-Molly-Mandy having Teacher to stay, then.

The next day was Saturday, and Teacher's furniture had come, and she was busy all day arranging it and getting the curtains and the pictures up. And Milly-Molly-Mandy with little-friend-Susan and Billy Blunt came in the afternoon to help. And they ran up and down

stairs, and fetched hammers and nails, and held things, and made themselves very useful indeed.

And at four o'clock Teacher sent Billy Blunt out to get some cakes from Mrs Hubble's shop, while the others laid the table in the pretty little sitting-room. And they had a nice kind of picnic, with Milly-Molly-Mandy and little-friend-Susan sharing a cup, and Billy Blunt having a saucer for a plate, because everything wasn't unpacked yet. And they all laughed and talked, and were as happy as anything. And when Teacher said it was time to send them all off home Milly-Molly-Mandy was so sorry to think Teacher wasn't coming to sleep in the spare room any more that she wanted to kiss Teacher without being asked. And she actually did it, too. And little-friend-Susan and Billy Blunt didn't look a bit surprised, either. And after that, somehow, it didn't seem to matter that Teacher was strict in school, for they knew that she was really just a very nice, usual sort of person inside all the time!

11

MILLY-MOLLY-MANDY
GOES TO A FETE

ONCE UPON A TIME, while Milly-Molly-Mandy was shopping in the village for Mother, she saw a poster on a board outside Mr Blunt's corn-shop. So she stopped to read it, and she found that there was to be a fête held in the playing-field, with sports and competitions for children, and other things for grown-ups. And while she was reading Billy Blunt looked out of the shop door.

Milly-Molly-Mandy said, "Hullo, Billy!"

And Billy Blunt grinned and said, "Hullo, Milly-Molly-Mandy!" and he came and looked at the poster too.

"When's the fête to be?" said Milly-Molly-Mandy, and Billy Blunt pointed with his toe to the date. And then he pointed to the words,

"Hundred-yard races, three-legged races, etc.," and said, "I'm going in for them."

"Are you?" said Milly-Molly-Mandy, and began to be interested. She thought a fête would be quite fun, and decided to ask Mother when she got home if she might go to it too.

A day or two later, as Milly-Molly-Mandy was swinging on the meadow gate after school, she saw someone running along in the middle of the road in a very steady, business-like fashion. And who should it be but Billy Blunt?

"Hullo, Billy! Where're you going?" said Milly-Molly-Mandy.

Billy Blunt slowed up and wiped his forehead, panting. "I'm getting into training," said Billy Blunt, "for the races."

Milly-Molly-Mandy thought that was a very good idea.

"I'm going to do some running every day," said Billy Blunt, "till the fête."

Milly-Molly-Mandy was sure Billy Blunt would win.

And then Billy Blunt asked if Milly-Molly-Mandy could count minutes, because it would be nice to have someone to time his running sometimes. Milly-Molly-Mandy couldn't, because she had never tried. But after that she practised counting minutes with the kitchen clock, till she got to know just about how fast to count sixty so that it was almost exactly a minute.

And the next day Billy Blunt stood right at one end of the meadow, by the nice white cottage with the thatched roof where Milly-Molly-Mandy lived, and Milly-Molly-Mandy stood at the other end. And when Billy Blunt shouted "Go!" and began running, Milly-Molly-Mandy shut her eyes tight so that she wouldn't think of anything else, and began counting steadily. And Billy Blunt reached her side in just over a minute and a half. They did it several times, but Billy Blunt couldn't manage to do it in less time.

After that they tied their ankles together – Billy Blunt's left and Milly-Molly-Mandy's right – with Billy Blunt's scarf, and practised running with three legs across the field. It was such fun, and Milly-Molly-Mandy shouted with laughter sometimes because they just couldn't help falling over. But Billy Blunt was rather solemn, and very keen to do it properly – though even he couldn't keep from letting out a laugh now and then, when they got very entangled.

By the time of the fête Billy Blunt was able to get across the meadow in a little over a minute, and their three-legged running was really quite good, so they were full of hopes for winning some prizes in the sports.

The day of the fête was nice and fine, even if not very warm. But, as Billy Blunt said, it was just as well to have it a bit cool for the sports. As it was Bank Holiday nearly everybody in the village turned up, paying their sixpences at the gate, and admiring the flags, and saying "Hullo!" or "How do you do?" to each other.

Milly-Molly-Mandy went with her Father and Mother and Grandpa and Grandma and Uncle and Aunty. And little-friend-Susan was there with her mother, who was also looking after Miss Muggins's niece Jilly, as Miss Muggins didn't care much for fêtes. And Mr Jakes, the Postman, was there with his wife; and Mr Rudge, the Blacksmith in his Sunday suit.

There were coconut shies (Uncle won a coconut), and throwing little hoops (three throws a penny) over things spread out on a table (Mother got a pocket comb, but she tried to get an alarm clock), and lots of other fun.

And then the Children's Sports began. Milly-Molly-Mandy paid a penny for a try at walking along a very narrow board to reach a red balloon at the other end, but she toppled off before she got it, and everybody laughed. (Miss Muggins' Jilly got a balloon.)

Then they entered for the three-legged race – little-friend-Susan and Miss Muggins's Jilly together, and Milly-Molly-Mandy and Billy Blunt (because they had practised), and a whole row of other boys and girls.

A man tied their ankles, and shouted "Go!" and off they all started, and everybody laughed, and couples kept stumbling and tumbling round, but Milly-Molly-Mandy and Billy Blunt careered steadily along till they reached the winning post!

Then everybody laughed and clapped like anything, and Billy Blunt pulled the string from round their ankles in a great hurry and cleared off, and Milly-Molly-Mandy had to take his box of chocolates for him, as well as her own.

Then there was the hundred yards race for boys. There was one rather shabbily dressed boy who had stood looking on at all the games, so Father asked him if he didn't want to join in, and he said he hadn't any money. So Father paid for him to join in the race, and he looked so pleased!

A man shouted "Go!" and off went all the boys in a mass – and how they did run! Milly-Molly-Mandy was so excited that she had to keep jumping up and down. But Billy Blunt presently got a little bit ahead of the others.

Off they all started

(Milly-Molly-Mandy held herself tight.) And then he got a little bit farther – and so did the shabby boy – only not so far as Billy Blunt. And then Billy Blunt saw him out of the corner of his eye as he ran, and then the race was over, and somehow the shabby boy had won. And he got a striped tin of toffee.

And Billy Blunt grinned at the shabby boy, who looked so happy hugging his tin of toffee, and asked him his name, and where he lived, and would he come and practise racing with him in the meadow next Saturday.

The next day, as Milly-Molly-Mandy and Billy Blunt and one or two others were coming home from school, they saw a big man with a suitcase waiting at the crossroads for the bus, which went every hour into the town. And just as the bus came in sight the man's hat blew off away down the road, ever such a distance. The man looked for a moment as if he didn't know what to do; and then he caught sight of them and shouted:

"Hi! – can any of you youngsters run?"

Milly-Molly-Mandy said, "Billy Blunt, can!" And instantly off went Billy Blunt down the

road in his best racing style. And just as the
bus pulled up at the stopping place, he picked
up the hat and came tearing back with it.

"I should just say you can run!" said the
man. "You've saved me an hour's wait for the
next bus and a whole lot of business besides."

"What a good thing you were in training!"
said Milly-Molly-Mandy to Billy Blunt, as the
bus went off.

"Huh! more sense, that,
than just racing," said
Billy Blunt, putting
his hair straight.

12

MILLY-MOLLY-MANDY
HAS A SURPRISE

ONCE UPON A TIME Milly-Molly-Mandy
was helping Mother to fetch some pots of jam
down from the little storeroom.

Father and Mother and Grandpa and
Grandma and Uncle and Aunty and Milly-
Molly-Mandy between them ate quite a lot of
jam, so Mother (who made all the jam) had to
keep the pots upstairs because the kitchen
cupboard wouldn't hold them all.

The little storeroom was up under the
thatched roof, and it had a little square window very near to the floor, and the ceiling
sloped away on each side so that Father or
Mother or Grandpa or Grandma or Uncle or
Aunty could stand upright only in the very

middle of the room. (But Milly-Molly-Mandy could stand upright anywhere in it.)

When Mother and Milly-Molly-Mandy had found the jams they wanted (strawberry jam and blackberry jam and ginger jam), Mother looked round the little storeroom and said, "It's a pity I haven't got somewhere else to keep my jam-pots!"

And Milly-Molly-Mandy said, "Why, Mother, I think this is a very nice place for jam-pots to live in!"

And Mother said, "Do you?"

But a few days later Father and Mother went up to the little storeroom together and took out all the jam-pots and all the shelves that held the jam-pots and Father stood them down in the new shed he was making outside the back door, while Mother started cleaning out the little storeroom.

Milly-Molly-Mandy helped by washing the little square window – "So that my jam-pots can see out!" Mother said.

The next day Milly-Molly-Mandy came upon Father in the barn, mixing colour-wash in a bucket. It was a pretty colour, just like a pale new primrose, and Milly-Molly-Mandy dabbled in it with a bit of stick for a while, and then she asked what it was for.

And Father said, "I'm going to do over the walls and ceiling of the little storeroom with it." And then he added, "Don't you think it will make the jam-pots feel nice and cheerful?"

And Milly-Molly-Mandy said she was sure the jam-pots would just love it! (It was such fun!)

A little while afterwards Mother sent Milly-Molly-Mandy to the village to buy a packet of green dye at Mr Smale the Grocer's shop. And then Mother dyed some old casement curtains a bright green for the little storeroom window. "Because," said Mother, "the window looks so bare from outside."

And while she was about it she said she might as well dye the coverlet on Milly-Molly-Mandy's little cot-bed (which stood in one corner of Father's and Mother's room), as the pattern had washed nearly white. So Milly-Molly-Mandy had a nice new bedspread, instead of a faded old one.

The next Saturday, when Grandpa came home from market, he brought with him in the back of the pony-trap a little chest of drawers, which he said he had "picked up cheap." He thought it might come in useful for keeping things in, in the little storeroom.

And Mother said, yes, it would come in very useful indeed. So (as it was rather shabby) Uncle, who had been painting the door of the new shed with apple-green paint, painted the little chest of drawers green too, so that it was a very pretty little chest of drawers indeed.

"Well," said Uncle, "that ought to make any jam-pot taste sweet!"

Milly-Molly-Mandy began to think the little storeroom would be almost too good just for jam-pots.

Then Aunty decided she and Uncle wanted a new mirror in their room, and she asked Mother if their little old one couldn't be stored up in the little storeroom. And when Mother said it could, Uncle said he might as well use up the last of the green paint, so that he could throw away the tin. So he painted the frame of the mirror green, and it looked a very pretty little mirror indeed.

"Jam-pots don't want to look at themselves," said Milly-Molly-Mandy. She thought the mirror looked much too pretty for the little storeroom.

"Oh well – a mirror helps to make the room lighter," said Mother.

Then Milly-Molly-Mandy came upon Grandma embroidering a pretty little wool bird on either end of a strip of coarse linen. It was a robin, with a brown back and a scarlet front. Milly-Molly-Mandy thought it *was* a pretty cloth: and she wanted to know what it was for.

And Grandma said, "I just thought it would look nice on the little chest of drawers in the little storeroom." And then she added, "It might amuse the jam-pots!"

And Milly-Molly-Mandy laughed, and begged Grandma to tell her what the pretty cloth really was for. But Grandma would only chuckle and say it was to amuse the jam-pots.

The next day, when Milly-Molly-Mandy came home from school, Mother said, "Milly-Molly-Mandy, we've got the little storeroom in order again. Now, would you please run up and fetch me a pot of jam?"

Milly-Molly-Mandy said, "Yes, Mother. What sort?"

And Father said, "Blackberry."

And Grandpa said, "Marrow-ginger."

And Grandma said, "Red-currant."

And Uncle said, "Strawberry."

And Aunty said, "Raspberry."

But Mother said, "Any sort you like, Milly-Molly-Mandy!"

Milly-Molly-Mandy thought something funny must be going to happen, for Father and Mother and Grandpa and Grandma and Uncle and Aunty all looked as if they had got a laugh down inside them. But she ran upstairs to the little storeroom.

And when she opened the door, ...she saw...

Her own little cot-bed with the green coverlet on, just inside. And the little square window with the green curtains blowing in the wind. And a yellow pot of nasturtiums on the sill. And the little green chest of drawers with the robin cloth on it. And the little green mirror hanging on the primrose wall, with Milly-Molly-Mandy's own face reflected in it.

And then Milly-Molly-Mandy knew that the little storeroom was to be her very own little bedroom, and she said, "Oh-h-h-h!" in a very

She said, "Oh-h-h-h!" in a very hushed voice

hushed voice, as she looked all round her room.

Then suddenly she tore downstairs back into the kitchen, and just hugged Father and Mother and Grandpa and Grandma and Uncle and Aunty; and they all said she was their favourite jam-pot and pretended to eat her up!

And Milly-Molly-Mandy didn't know how to wait till bedtime, because she was so eager to go to sleep in the little room that was her Very Own!

13

MILLY-MOLLY-MANDY
GOES TO A CONCERT

ONCE UPON A TIME Milly-Molly-Mandy was going to a grown-up concert with Father and Mother and Grandpa and Grandma and Uncle and Aunty. (They had all got their tickets.)

It was to be held in the Village Institute at seven o'clock, and it wouldn't be over until quite nine o'clock, which was lovely and late for Milly-Molly-Mandy. But you see this wasn't like an ordinary concert, where people you didn't know sang and did things.

It was a quite extra specially important concert, for Aunty was going to play on the piano on the platform, and the young lady who helped Mrs Hubble in her baker's shop was going to sing, and some other people whom

Milly-Molly-Mandy had heard spoken of were
going to do things too. So it was very exciting
indeed.

Aunty had a new mauve silk scarf for her
neck, and a newly trimmed hat, and her handkerchief was sprinkled with the lavender water
that Milly-Molly-Mandy had given her last
Christmas.

Milly-Molly-Mandy felt so proud that it was
being used for such a special occasion. (Aunty
put a drop on Milly-Molly-Mandy's own handkerchief too.)

When they had all got into their best clothes
and shoes, they said goodbye to Toby the dog

121

and Topsy the cat, and started off for the village — Father and Mother and Grandpa and Grandma and Uncle and Aunty and Milly-Molly-Mandy. And they as nearly as possible forgot to take the tickets with them off the mantelpiece! But Mother remembered just in time.

There were several people already in their seats when Father and Mother and Grandpa and Grandma and Uncle and Aunty and Milly-Molly-Mandy got to the Institute. Mr and Mrs Hubble and the young lady who helped them were just in front, and Mr and Mrs Blunt and Mr and Mrs Moggs (little-friend-Susan's father and mother) were just behind (Billy Blunt and little-friend-Susan weren't there, but then they hadn't got an aunty who was going to play on the platform, so it wasn't so important for them to be up late).

The platform looked very nice, with plants in crinkly green paper. And the piano was standing there, all ready for Aunty. People were coming in very fast, and it wasn't long before the hall was full, everybody was talking and rustling programmes. Then people started clapping, and Milly-Molly-Mandy saw that some ladies and gentlemen with violins and things were going up steps on to the platform, with very solemn faces. A lady hit one or two notes on the piano, and the people with violins played a lot of funny noises without taking any notice of each other (Mother said they were "tuning up"). And then they all started off playing properly, and the concert had begun.

Milly-Molly-Mandy did enjoy it. She clapped as hard as ever she could, and so did everybody else, when the music stopped. After that people sang one at a time, or a lot at a time, or played the piano, and one man sang a funny song (which made Milly-Molly-Mandy laugh and everybody else too).

But Milly-Molly-Mandy was longing for the time to come for Aunty to play.

She was just asking Mother in a whisper when Aunty was going to play, when she heard a queer little sound, just like a dog walking on the wooden floor. And she looked round and saw people at the back of the hall glancing down here and there, smiling and pointing.

And presently what should she feel but a

cold, wet nose on her leg, and what should she see but a white, furry object coming out from under her chair.

And there was Toby the dog (without a ticket), looking just as pleased with himself as he could be for having found them!

Milly-Molly-Mandy was very shocked at him and so was Mother. She said "Naughty Toby!" in a whisper, and Father pushed him under the seat and made him lie down. They couldn't disturb the concert by taking him out just then.

So there Toby the dog stayed and heard the concert without a ticket; and now and then Milly-Molly-Mandy put down her hand and Toby the dog licked it and half got up to wag his tail. But Father said, "Ssh!" so Milly-

Molly-Mandy put her hand back in her lap, and Toby the dog settled down again. But they liked being near each other.

Then the time came for the young lady who helped Mrs Hubble to sing, and Aunty to play for her. So the young lady got up and dropped her handbag, and Aunty got up and dropped her music (it made Toby the dog jump!). But they were picked up again, and then Aunty and the young lady went up on to the platform.

And who do you think went up with them?

Why, Toby the dog! Looking just as if he thought Aunty had meant him to follow!

Everybody laughed, and Aunty pointed to Toby the dog to go down again. But Toby the dog didn't seem to understand, and he got behind the piano and wouldn't come out.

So Aunty had to play and the young lady to sing with Toby the dog peeping out now and then from behind the piano, and everybody tried not to notice him, lest it should make them laugh.

But still Aunty played beautifully and the young lady sang, and Milly-Molly-Mandy clapped as hard as she could, and so did everybody else when the song was finished. In fact, they all clapped so loud that Toby the dog gave a surprised bark, and everybody laughed again.

They had another try then to get Toby the dog off the platform, but Toby the dog wouldn't come.

Then Father said, "Milly-Molly-Mandy, you go and see if you can get him."

So Milly-Molly-Mandy slipped off her seat, past the people's knees, and climbed up the steps on to the platform (in front of all the audience).

And she said, "Toby, come here!" round the corner of the piano, and Toby the dog put out his nose and sniffed her hand, and Milly-Molly-Mandy was able to catch hold of his collar and pull him out.

She walked right across the platform with Toby the dog in her arms, and everybody laughed, and somebody (I think it was the Blacksmith) called out, "Bravo! Encore!" and clapped.

And Milly-Molly-Mandy (feeling very hot) hurried down the steps, with Toby the dog

She walked right across the platform

licking all over one side of her cheek and hair.

There was only a little bit of the concert to come after that, so Milly-Molly-Mandy stood at the back of the hall with Toby the dog till it was finished. Then everybody started crowding to the door. Most of them smiled at Milly-Molly-Mandy and Toby the dog as they stood waiting for Father and Mother and Grandpa and Grandma and Uncle and Aunty to come.

Mr Jakes the Postman, passing with Mrs Jakes, said, "Well, well! I didn't expect to see you turning out a public character just yet awhile, young lady." And Milly-Molly-Mandy laughed with Mr Jakes.

Then Mr Rudge, the Blacksmith, passed, and he said solemnly, "You and Toby gave us a very fine performance indeed. If I'd known beforehand I'd have sent you up a bouquet each." Milly-Molly-Mandy liked the Blacksmith – he was a nice man.

"Well," said Aunty, as they all walked home together in the dark, "I think if we'd known Toby was going to perform up on the platform tonight, we'd have given him a bath and a new collar first!"

14

MILLY-MOLLY-MANDY'S
MOTHER GOES AWAY

ONCE UPON A TIME Milly-Molly-Mandy's
Mother went away from the nice white cottage
with the thatched roof for a whole fortnight's
holiday.

Milly-Molly-Mandy's Mother hardly ever
went away for holidays – in fact, Milly-Molly-
Mandy could only remember her going away
once before, a long time ago (and that was
only for two days).

Mrs Hooker, Mother's friend in the next
town, invited her. Mrs Hooker wanted to have
a holiday by the sea, and she didn't want to go
alone, as it isn't so much fun, so she wrote and
asked Mother to come with her.

When Mother read the letter first, she said it
was very kind of Mrs Hooker, but she couldn't

possibly go, as she didn't see how ever Father and Grandpa and Grandma and Uncle and Aunty and Milly-Molly-Mandy would get on without her to cook dinners for them, and wash clothes for them, and see after things.

But Aunty said she could manage to do the cooking and the washing, somehow; and Grandma said she could do Aunty's sweeping and dusting; and Milly-Molly-Mandy said she would help all she knew how; and Father and Grandpa and Uncle said they wouldn't be fussy, or make any more work than they could help.

And then they all begged Mother to write to Mrs Hooker and accept. So Mother did, and she was quite excited (and so was Milly-Molly-Mandy for her!).

Then Mother bought a new hat and a blouse and a sunshade, and she packed them in her trunk with all her best things (Milly-Molly-Mandy helping).

And then she kissed Grandpa and Grandma

and Uncle and Aunty goodbye, and hugged Milly-Molly-Mandy. And then Father drove her in the pony-trap to the next town to the station to meet Mrs Hooker and go with her by train to the sea. (She kissed Father goodbye at the station.)

And so Father and Grandpa and Grandma and Uncle and Aunty and Milly-Molly-Mandy had to manage as best they could in the nice white cottage with the thatched roof for a whole fortnight without Mother. It did feel queer.

Milly-Molly-Mandy kept forgetting, and she would run in from school to tell Mother all about something, and find it was Aunty in Mother's apron bending over the kitchen stove instead of Mother herself. And Father would put his head in at the kitchen door and say, "Polly, will you –" and then suddenly remember that "Polly" was having a lovely holiday by the sea (Polly was Mother's other name, of course). And they felt so pleased when they remembered, but it did seem a long time to wait till she came back.

Then one day Father said, "I've got a plan!

Don't you think it would be a good idea, while Polly's away, if we were to . . . "

And then Father told them all his plan; and Grandpa and Grandma and Uncle and Aunty thought it was a very fine plan, and so did Milly-Molly-Mandy. (But I mustn't tell you what it was, because it was to be a surprise, and you know how secrets do get about once you start telling them! But I'll just tell you this, that they made the kitchen and the scullery and the passage outside the kitchen most dreadfully untidy, so that nothing was in its proper place, and they had to have meals like picnics, only not so nice – though Milly-Molly-Mandy thought it quite fun.)

Well, they all worked awfully hard at the plan in all their spare time, and nobody really minded having things all upset, because it was such fun to think how surprised Mother would be when she came back!

Then another day Grandpa said: "There's something I've been meaning to do for some time, to please Polly; I guess it would be a good plan to set about it now. It is . . . "

And then Grandpa told them all his plan;

and Father and Grandma and Uncle and
Aunty thought it was a very fine plan, and so
did Milly-Molly-Mandy. (But I mustn't tell
you what it was! – though I will just tell you
this, that Grandpa was very busy digging up
things in the garden and planting them again,
and bringing things home in a box at the back
of the pony-trap on market day. And Milly-
Molly-Mandy helped him all she could.)

Then Uncle had a plan, and Father and
Grandpa and Grandma and Aunty thought it
was a very fine plan, and so did Milly-Molly-
Mandy. (It's a secret, remember! – but I will
just tell you this, that Uncle got a lot of bits of
wood and nails and a hammer, and he was very
busy in the evening after he had shut up his
chickens for the night – which he called
"putting them to bed.")

Then Grandma and Aunty had a plan, and
Father and Grandpa and Uncle thought it was
a very fine plan, and so did Milly-Molly-
Mandy. (But I can only just tell you this, that
Grandma and Aunty and Milly-Molly-Mandy,
who helped too, made themselves very untidy
and dusty indeed, and nobody had any cakes

133

for tea at all that week, what with Aunty being so busy and the kitchen so upset. But nobody really minded, because it was such fun to think how pleased Mother would be when she came back!)

And then the day arrived when Mother was to return home!

They had all been working so hard in the nice white cottage with the thatched roof that the two weeks had simply flown. But they had just managed to get things straight again, and Aunty had baked a cake for tea, and Milly-Molly-Mandy had put flowers in all the vases.

When Father helped Mother down from the pony-trap it almost didn't seem as if it could be Mother at first; but of course it was! – only she had on her new hat, and she was so brown with sitting on the beach, and so very pleased to be home again!

She kissed them all round and just hugged Milly-Molly-Mandy!

And then they led her indoors.

And directly Mother got inside the doorway – she saw a beautiful new passage, all clean and painted! And she was surprised!

Then she went upstairs and took off her things, and came back down into the kitchen. And directly Mother got inside the door – she saw a beautiful new kitchen, all clean and sunny, with the ceiling whitewashed and the walls freshly painted! And she was surprised!

When they had had tea (Aunty's cake was very good, though not quite like Mother's) she helped to carry the cups and plates out into the scullery. And directly Mother got through the doorway – she saw a beautiful new scullery, all clean and white-washed! And she was surprised!

She put the cups down on the draining board, and directly she looked out of the window – she saw a beautiful new flower garden

And she was surprised!

just outside, and a rustic trellis-work hiding the dustbin. And she was surprised!

Then Mother went upstairs to unpack. And when her trunk was cleared, Grandpa carried it up to the attic and Mother went first to open the door. And directly she opened it – Mother saw a beautifully tidy, spring-cleaned attic!

And then Mother couldn't say anything, but that they were all very dear, naughty people to have worked so hard while she was being lazy! And Father and Grandpa and Grandma and Uncle and Aunty and Milly-Molly-Mandy were all very pleased, and said they liked being naughty!

Then Mother brought out the presents she had got for them. And what do you think Milly-Molly-Mandy's present was (besides some shells which Mother had picked up on the sand)?

It was a beautiful little blue dressing-gown, which Mother had sewed and sewed for her while she sat on the beach and under her new sunshade with Mrs Hooker listening to the waves splashing!

Then Father and Grandpa and Grandma

and Uncle and Aunty and Milly-Molly-Mandy all said Mother was very naughty to have worked when she might have been having a nice lazy time!

But Mother said she liked being naughty too! – and Milly-Molly-Mandy was so pleased with her new little blue dressing-gown that she couldn't help wearing it straight away!

And then Mother put on her apron and insisted on setting to work to make them something nice for supper, so that she should feel she was really at home.

For it had been a perfect holiday, said Mother, but it was really like having another one to come home again to them all at the nice white cottage with the thatched roof.

15

MILLY-MOLLY-MANDY
GOES TO THE SEA

Once upon a time – what do you think? –
Milly-Molly-Mandy was going to be taken to
the seaside!

Milly-Molly-Mandy had never seen the sea
in all her life before, and ever since Mother
came back from her seaside holiday with her
friend Mrs Hooker, and told Milly-Molly-
Mandy about the splashy waves and the sand
and the little crabs, Milly-Molly-Mandy had
just longed to go there herself.

Father and Mother and Grandpa and
Grandma and Uncle and Aunty just longed for
her to go too, because they knew she would
like it so much. But they were all so busy, and
then, you know, holidays cost quite a lot of
money.

So Milly-Molly-Mandy played 'seaside' instead, by the little brook in the meadow, with little-friend-Susan and Billy Blunt and the shells Mother had brought home for her. (And it was a very nice game indeed, but still Milly-Molly-Mandy did wish sometimes that it could be the real sea!)

Then one day little-friend-Susan went with her mother and baby sister to stay with a relation who let lodgings by the sea. And little-friend-Susan wrote Milly-Molly-Mandy a postcard saying how lovely it was, and how she did wish Milly-Molly-Mandy was there; and Mrs Moggs wrote Mother a postcard saying couldn't some of them manage to come down just for a day excursion, one Saturday?

Father and Mother and Grandpa and Grandma and Uncle and Aunty thought something really ought to be done about that, and they talked it over, while Milly-Molly-Mandy listened with all her ears.

But Father said he couldn't go, because he had to get his potatoes up; Mother said she couldn't go because it was baking day, and, besides, she had just had a lovely seaside holiday; Grandpa said he couldn't go, because it was market day; Grandma said she wasn't really very fond of train journeys; Uncle said he oughtn't to leave his cows and chickens.

But then they all said Aunty could quite well leave the sweeping and dusting for that one day.

So Aunty only said it seemed too bad that she should have all the fun. And then she and Milly-Molly-Mandy hugged each other, because it was so very exciting.

Milly-Molly-Mandy ran off to tell Billy Blunt at once, because she felt she would burst if she didn't tell someone. And Billy Blunt did wish he could be going too, but his father and mother were always busy.

Milly-Molly-Mandy told Aunty, and Aunty said, "Tell Billy Blunt to ask his mother to let him come with us, and I'll see after him!"

So Billy Blunt did, and Mrs Blunt said it was very kind of Aunty and she'd be glad to let him go.

Milly-Molly-Mandy hoppity-skipped like anything, because she was so very pleased; and Billy Blunt was very pleased too, though he

didn't hoppity-skip, because he always thought
he was too old for such doings (but he wasn't
really!).

So now they were able to plan together for
Saturday, which made it much more fun.

Mother had an old bathing-dress which she
cut down to fit Milly-Molly-Mandy, and the
bits over she made into a flower for the shoulder (and it looked a very smart bathing-dress
indeed). Billy Blunt borrowed a swimming-
suit from another boy at school (but it hadn't
any flower on the shoulder, of course not!).

Then Billy Blunt said to Milly-Molly-
Mandy, "If you've got swimming-suits you
ought to swim. We'd better practise."

But Milly-Molly-Mandy
said, "We haven't got
enough water."

Billy Blunt said,
"Practise in air, then –
better than nothing."

So they fetched two old
boxes from the barn out into the yard, and
then lay on them (on their fronts) and spread
out their arms and kicked with their legs just

as if they were swimming. And when Uncle came along to fetch a wheelbarrow he said it really made him feel quite cool to see them!

He showed them how to turn their hands properly, and kept calling out, "Steady! Steady! Not so fast!" as he watched them.

And then Uncle lay on his front on the box and showed them how (and he looked so funny!), and then they tried again, and Uncle said it was better that time.

So they practised until they were quite out of breath. And then they pretended to dive off the boxes, and they splashed and swallowed mouthfuls of air and swam races to the gate and shivered and dried themselves with old sacks – and it was almost as much fun as if it were real water!

Well, Saturday came at last, and Aunty and Milly-Molly-Mandy met Billy Blunt at nine o'clock by the crossroads. And then they went in the red bus to the station in the next town. And then they went in the train, rumpty-te-tump, rumpty-te-tump, all the way down to the sea.

And you can't imagine how exciting it was,

when they got out at last, to walk down a road knowing they would see the real sea at the bottom! Milly-Molly-Mandy got so excited that she didn't want to look till they were up quite close.

So Billy Blunt (who had seen it once before) pulled her along right on to the edge of the sand, and then he said suddenly, "Now look!"

And Milly-Molly-Mandy looked.

And there was the sea, all jumping with sparkles in the sunshine, as far as ever you could see. And little-friend-Susan, with bare legs and frock tucked up, came tearing over the sand to meet them from where Mrs Moggs and Baby Moggs were sitting by a wooden breakwater.

Wasn't it fun!

They took off their shoes and their socks and their hats, and they wanted to take off their clothes and bathe, but Aunty said they must have dinner first. So they sat round and ate sandwiches and cake and fruit which Aunty had brought in a basket. And the Moggs' had theirs too out of a basket.

Then they played in the sand with Baby Moggs (who liked having her legs buried), and paddled a bit and found crabs (they didn't take them away from the water, though).

And then Aunty and Mrs Moggs said they might bathe now if they wanted to. So (as it was a very quiet sort of beach) Milly-Molly-Mandy undressed behind Aunty, and little-friend-Susan undressed behind Mrs Moggs, and Billy Blunt undressed behind the breakwater.

And then they ran right into the water in their bathing-dresses. (And little-friend-Susan thought Milly-Molly-Mandy's bathing-dress was smart, with the flower on the shoulder!)

But, dear me! Water-swimming feels so different from land-swimming, and Milly-Molly-

They ran right into the water in their bathing dresses

Mandy couldn't manage at all well with the little waves splashing at her all the time. Billy Blunt swished about in the water with a very grim face, and looked exactly as if he were swimming; but when Milly-Molly-Mandy asked him, he said, "No! My arms swim, but my legs only walk!"

It was queer, for it had seemed quite easy in the barnyard.

But they went on pretending and pretending to swim until Aunty called them out. And then they dried themselves with towels and got into their clothes again; and Billy Blunt said, well, anyhow, he supposed they were just that much nearer swimming properly than they were before; and Milly-Molly-Mandy said she supposed next time they might p'r'aps be able to lift their feet off the ground for a minute at any rate; and little-friend-Susan said she was sure she had swallowed a shrimp! (But that was only her fun!)

Then they played and explored among the rock-pools and had tea on the sand. And after tea Mrs Moggs and Baby Moggs and little-friend-Susan walked with them back to the station; and Aunty and Milly-Molly-Mandy and Billy Blunt went in the train, rumpty-te-tump, rumpty-te-tump, all the way home again.

And Milly-Molly-Mandy was so sleepy when she got to the nice white cottage with the thatched roof that she had only just time to kiss Father and Mother and Grandpa and Grandma and Uncle and Aunty goodnight and get into bed before she fell fast asleep.

16

MILLY-MOLLY-MANDY
MINDS A BABY

ONCE UPON A TIME Milly-Molly-Mandy
had to mind a tiny little baby.

It was the funniest, tiny little baby you could
possibly imagine, and Milly-Molly-Mandy had
to mind it because there didn't seem to be any-
body else to do so. She couldn't find its mother
or its father or any of its relations, so she had
to take it home and look after it herself
(because, of course, you can't leave a tiny little
baby alone in a wood, with no one anywhere
about to look after it).

And this is how it happened.

Milly-Molly-Mandy wanted some acorn
cups (which are useful for making dolls' bowls,
and wheels for matchbox carts, and all that
sort of thing, you know). So, as little-friend-

Susan was busy looking after her baby sister, Milly-Molly-Mandy went off to the woods with just Toby the dog to look for some.

While she was busy looking she heard a loud chirping noise. And Milly-Molly-Mandy said to herself, "I wonder what sort of bird that is?" And then she found a ripe blackberry, and forgot about the chirping noise.

After a time Milly-Molly-Mandy said to herself, "How that bird does keep on chirping?" And then Toby the dog found a rabbit hole, and Milly-Molly-Mandy forgot again about the chirping noise.

After some more time Milly-Molly-Mandy said to herself, "That bird sounds as if it wants something." And then Milly-Molly-Mandy went towards a brambly clearing in the wood from which the chirping noise seemed to come.

But when she got there the chirping noise

didn't seem to come from a tree, but from a
low bramble bush. And when she got to the
low bramble bush the chirping noise stopped.

Milly-Molly-Mandy thought that was
because it was frightened of her. So she said
out loud, "It's all right – don't be frightened. It's
only me!" just as kindly as she could, and then
she poked about in among the bramble bush.
But she couldn't find anything, except thorns.

And then, quite
suddenly, lying in
the grass on the
other side of the
bramble bush,
Milly-Molly-
Mandy and
Toby the dog

together found what had been making all the
chirping noise. It was so frightened that it had
rolled itself into a tight little prickly ball, no
bigger than the penny india rubber ball which
Milly-Molly-Mandy had bought at Miss
Muggins's shop the day before.

For what DO you think it was? A little tiny
weeny baby hedgehog!

Milly-Molly-Mandy was excited! And so was Toby the dog! Milly-Molly-Mandy had to say, "No, Toby! Be quiet, Toby!" very firmly indeed. And then she picked up the baby hedgehog in a bracken leaf (because it was a very prickly baby, though it was so small), and she could just see its little soft nose quivering among its prickles.

Then Milly-Molly-Mandy looked about to find its nest (for, of course, she didn't want to take it away from its family), but she couldn't find it. And then the baby began squeaking again for its mother, but its mother didn't come.

So at last Milly-Molly-Mandy said comfortingly, "Never mind, darling – I'll take you home and look after you!"

So Milly-Molly-Mandy carried the baby hedgehog between her two hands very carefully; and it unrolled itself a bit and quivered its little soft nose over her fingers as if it hoped they might be good to eat, and it squeaked and squeaked, because it was very hungry. So Milly-Molly-Mandy hurried all she could, and Toby the dog capered along at her side and at last they got home to the nice white cottage with the thatched roof.

Father and Mother and Grandpa and Grandma and Uncle and Aunty were all very interested indeed.

Mother put a saucer of milk on the stove to warm, and then they tried to feed the baby. But it was too little to lap from a saucer, and it was too little even to lick from Milly-Molly-Mandy's finger. So at last they had to wait until it opened its mouth to squeak and then squirt drops of warm milk into it with Father's fountain pen filler!

After that the baby felt a bit happier, and Milly-Molly-Mandy made it a nest in a little box of hay. But when she put it in it squeaked and squeaked again for its nice warm mother till Milly-Molly-Mandy put her hand in the box; and then it snuggled up against it and went to sleep. And Milly-Molly-Mandy stood there and chuckled softly to herself, because it felt so funny being mistaken for Mrs Hedgehog! (She quite liked it!)

When Father and Grandpa and Uncle came in to dinner the baby woke and began squeaking again. So Uncle picked it up in his big hand to have a look at it, while Milly-Molly-Mandy ran for more milk and the fountain pen filler.

And the baby squeaked so loudly that Uncle said, "Hul-lo, Horace! What's all this noise about!" And Milly-Molly-Mandy was pleased, because "Horace" just seemed to suit the baby hedgehog, and no one knew what its mother had named it (but I don't suppose it was Horace!).

Milly-Molly-Mandy was kept very busy all that day feeding Horace every hour or two. He was so prickly that she had to wrap him round in an old handkerchief first – and he looked the funniest little baby in a white shawl you ever did see!

When bedtime came Milly-Molly-Mandy wanted to take the hedgehog's box up to her little room with her. But Mother said no, he would be all right in the kitchen till morning. So they gave him a hot bottle to snuggle against (it was an ink bottle, wrapped in flannel), and then Milly-Molly-Mandy went off to bed.

But being "mother" even to a hedgehog is a

They were all very interested indeed

very important sort of job, and in the night Milly-Molly-Mandy woke up and thought of Horace, and wondered if he felt lonely in his new home.

And she creepy-crept in the dark to the top of the stairs and listened.

And after a time she heard a tiny little "Squeak! Squeak!" coming from the kitchen. So she hurried and pulled on her dressing-gown and her bedroom slippers, and then she hurried and creepy-crept in the dark downstairs into the kitchen, and carefully lit the candle on the dresser.

And then she fed Horace and talked to him in a comfortable whisper, so that he didn't feel lonely any more. And then she put him back to bed and blew out the candle, and creepy-crept in the dark upstairs to her own little bed. (And it did feel so nice and warm to get into again!)

Next day Horace learned to open his mouth when he felt the fountain pen filler touch it (he couldn't see, because his eyes weren't open yet

– just like a baby puppy or kitten). And quite soon he learned to suck away at the filler just as if it were a proper baby's bottle! And he grew and he grew, and in a week's time his eyes were open. And soon he grew little teeth, and could gobble bread and milk out of an egg-cup, and sometimes a little bit of meat or banana.

He was quite a little-boy hedgehog now,  instead of a little baby one, and Milly-Molly-Mandy didn't need to get up in the night any more to feed him.

Milly-Molly-Mandy was very proud of him, and when little-friend-Susan used to say she had to hurry home after school to look after her baby sister, Milly-Molly-Mandy used to say she had to hurry too to look after the baby Horace. She used to give him walks in the garden, and laugh at his funny little back legs and tiny tail as he waddled about, nosing the ground. When Toby the dog barked he would roll himself up

into a prickly ball in a second; but he soon
came out again, and would run to Milly-Molly-
Mandy's hand when she called "Horace!" (He
was quite happy with her for a mother.)

One day Horace got out of his hay-box in
the kitchen, and they couldn't find him for a
long time, though they all looked – Father and
Mother and Grandpa and Grandma and Uncle
and Aunty and Milly-Molly-Mandy. But at last
where do you think they found him? – in the
larder!

"Well!" said Uncle, "Horace knows how to
look after himself all right now!"

After that Horace's bed was put out in the
barn, and Milly-Molly-Mandy would take his
little basin of bread and milk out to him, and
stay and play till it got too chilly.

And then, one frosty morning, they couldn't
find Horace anywhere, though they all looked –
Father and Mother and Grandpa and Grandma
and Uncle and Aunty and Milly-Molly-Mandy.
But at last, a day or two after, Grandpa was
pulling out some hay for the pony Twinkletoes,
when what do you think he found! A little ball
of prickles cuddled up deep in the hay!

Horace had gone to sleep for the winter, like the proper little hedgehog he was! (Grandpa said that sort of going to sleep was called "hibernating".)

So Milly-Molly-Mandy put the hay with the prickly ball inside it into a large box in the barn, with a little bowl of water near by (in case Horace should wake up and want a drink).

And there she left him (sleeping soundly while the cold winds blew and the snows fell) until he should wake up in the spring and come out to play with her again!

(And that's a true story!)

17

MILLY-MOLLY-MANDY GOES

ON AN EXPEDITION

ONCE UPON A TIME it was a Monday-bank-holiday. Milly-Molly-Mandy had been looking forward to this Monday-bank-holiday for a long time, more than a week, for she and Billy Blunt had been planning to go for a long fishing expedition on that day.

It was rather exciting.

They were to get up very early, and take their dinners with them, and their rods and lines and jam-jars, and go off all on their own along by the brook, and not be back until quite late in the day.

Milly-Molly-Mandy went to bed the night before with all the things she wanted for the expedition arranged beside her bed – a new little tin mug (to drink out of), and a bottle (for drinking water), and a large packet of bread-and-butter and an egg and a banana (for her dinner), and a jam-jar (to carry the fish in), and a little green fishing net (to catch them with), and some string and a safety-pin (which it is always useful to have), and her school satchel (to put things in). For when you are going off for the whole day you want quite a lot of things with you.

When Milly-Molly-Mandy woke up on Monday-bank-holiday morning she thought to herself, "Oh, dear! It is a grey sort of day – I do hope it isn't going to rain!"

But anyhow she knew she was going to enjoy herself, and she jumped up and washed and dressed and put on her hat and the satchel strap over her shoulder.

And then the sunshine came creeping over the trees outside, and Milly-Molly-Mandy saw that it had only been a grey day because she was up before the sun – and she felt a sort of little skip inside, because she was so very sure she was going to enjoy herself!

Just then there came a funny gritty sound like a handful of earth on the window pane, and when she put her head out there was Billy Blunt, eating a large piece of bread-and-butter and grinning up at her, looking very businesslike with rod and line and jam-jar and bulging satchel.

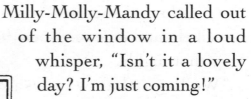

Milly-Molly-Mandy called out of the window in a loud whisper, "Isn't it a lovely day? I'm just coming!"

And Billy Blunt called back in a loud whisper, "Come on! Hurry up! It's getting late."

So Milly-Molly-Mandy hurried up like anything,

and picked up her things and ran creeping
downstairs, past Father's and Mother's room,
and Grandpa's and Grandma's room, and
Uncle's and Aunty's room. And she filled her
bottle at the tap in the scullery, and took up
the thick slice of bread-and-butter which
Mother had left between two plates ready for
her breakfast, and unlocked the back door and
slipped out into the fresh morning air.

And there they were, off on their Monday-
bank-holiday expedition!

"Isn't it lovely!" said Milly-Molly-Mandy,
with a little hop.

"Umm! Come on!" said Billy Blunt.

So they went out of the back gate and across
the meadow to the brook, walking very businesslikely and enjoying their bread-and-butter
very thoroughly.

"We'll go that way," said Billy Blunt,
"because that's the way we don't generally go."

"And when we come to a nice place we'll
fish," said Milly-Molly-Mandy.

"But that won't be for a long way yet," said
Billy Blunt.

So they went on walking very businesslikely

Off on their Monday bank-holiday expedition

(they had eaten their bread-and-butter by this time) until they had left the nice white cottage with the thatched roof a long way behind, and the sun was shining down quite hotly.

"It seems like a real expedition when you have the whole day to do it in, doesn't it?" said Milly-Molly-Mandy. "I wonder what the time is now!"

"Not time for dinner yet," said Billy Blunt. "But I could eat it."

"So could I," said Milly-Molly-Mandy. "Let's have a drink of water." So they each had a little tin mug full of water, and drank it very preciously to make it last, as the bottle didn't hold much.

The brook was too muddy and weedy for drinking, but it was a very interesting brook. One place, where it had got rather blocked up, was just full of tadpoles – they caught ever so many with their hands and put them in the jam-jars, and watched them swim about and wiggle their little black tails and open and shut their little black mouths. Then farther on were lots of stepping-stones in the stream, and Milly-Molly-Mandy and Billy Blunt had a fine time scrambling about from one to another.

Billy Blunt slipped once, with one foot into the water, so he took off his boots and socks and tied them round his neck. And it looked so nice that Milly-Molly-Mandy took off one boot and sock and tried it too. But the water and the stones were so-o cold that she put them on again, and just tried to be fairly careful how she went. But even so she slipped once, and caught her frock on a branch and pulled the button off, and had to fasten it together with a safety-pin. (So wasn't it a good thing she had brought one with her?)

Presently they came to a big flat mossy stone beside the brook. And Milly-Molly-Mandy said, "That's where we ought to eat our dinners, isn't it? I wonder what the time is now!"

Billy Blunt looked round and considered; and then he said, "Somewhere about noon, I should say. Might think about eating soon, as we had breakfast early. Less to carry, too."

And Milly-Molly-Mandy said, "Let's spread it out all ready, anyhow! It's a lovely place here."

So they laid the food out on the flat stone,

with the bottle of water and little tin mug in the middle, and it looked so good and they felt so hungry that, of course, they just had to set to and eat it all up straight away.

And it did taste nice!

And the little black tadpoles in the glass jam-jars beside them swam round and round, and wiggled their little black tails and opened and shut their little black mouths; till at last Milly-Molly-Mandy said, "We've taken them away from their dinners, haven't we? Let's put them back now."

And Billy Blunt said, "Yes. We'll want the pots for real fishes soon."

So they emptied the tadpoles back into the brook where they wiggled away at once to their meals.

"Look! There's a fish!" cried Milly-Molly-Mandy, pointing. And Billy Blunt hurried and fetched his rod and line, and settled to fishing in real earnest.

Milly-Molly-Mandy went a little farther down-stream, and poked about with her net in the water; and soon she caught a fish, and put it in her jam-jar, and ran to show it to Billy

Blunt. And Billy Blunt said, "Huh!" But he said it wasn't proper fishing without a rod and line, so it didn't really count.

But Milly-Molly-Mandy liked it quite well that way, all the same.

So they fished and they fished along the banks and sometimes they saw quite big fish, two or three inches long, and Billy Blunt got quite excited and borrowed Milly-Molly-Mandy's net; and they got a number of fish in their jam-jars.

"Oh, don't you wish we'd brought our teas too, so we could stay here a long, long time?" said Milly-Molly-Mandy.

"Umm," said Billy Blunt. "We ought to have done. Expect we'll have to be getting back soon."

So at last as they got hungry, and thirsty too (having finished all the bottle of water), they began to pack up their things and Billy Blunt put on his socks and boots. And they tramped all the way back, scrambling up and down the banks, and jumping the stepping-stones.

When they got near home Milly-Molly-Mandy said doubtfully, "What about our fishes?"

And Billy Blunt said, "We don't really want 'em now, do we? We only wanted a fishing expedition."

So they counted how many there were (there were fifteen), and then emptied them back into the brook, where they darted off at once to their meals.

And Milly-Molly-Mandy and Billy Blunt went on up through the meadow to the nice white cottage with the thatched roof, feeling very hungry, and hoping they weren't too badly late for tea.

And when they got in Father and Mother and Grandpa and Grandma and Uncle and

Aunty were all sitting at table, just finishing – what do you think?

Why, their midday dinner!

Milly-Molly-Mandy and Billy Blunt couldn't think how it had happened. But when you get up so very early to go on fishing expeditions, and get so very hungry, well, it is rather difficult to reckon the time properly!

18

MILLY-MOLLY-MANDY
HELPS TO THATCH A ROOF

ONCE UPON A TIME it was a very blustery night, so very blustery that it woke Milly-Molly-Mandy right up several times.

Milly-Molly-Mandy's little attic bedroom was just under the thatched roof, so she could hear the wind blowing in the thatch, as well as rattling her little low window, and even shaking her door.

Milly-Molly-Mandy had to pull the bed-clothes well over her ears to shut out some of the noise before she could go to sleep at all, and so did Father and Mother and Grandpa and Grandma and Uncle and Aunty, in their bedrooms. It was so very blustery.

The next morning, when Milly-Molly-Mandy woke up properly, the wind was still very blustery, though it didn't sound quite so loud as it did in the dark.

Milly-Molly-Mandy sat up in her little bed, thinking, "What a noisy night it was!" And she looked toward her little low window to see if it were raining.

But what do you think she saw? Why, lots of long bits of straw dangling and swaying just outside from the edge of the thatched roof above. And when she got up and looked out of her little low window she saw – why! – lots of long bits of straw lying all over the grass, and all over the flower-beds, and all over the hedge!

Milly-Molly-Mandy stared round, thinking, "It's been raining straw in the night!"

And then she thought some more. And suddenly she said right out loud, "Ooh! The wind's blowing our nice thatched roof off!"

And then Milly-Molly-Mandy didn't wait to think any longer, but ran barefooted down into Father's and Mother's room, calling out, "Ooh! Father and Mother! The wind's blowing our nice thatched roof off, and it's lying all over the garden!"

Then Father jumped out of bed, and put his boots on his bare feet, and his big coat over his pyjamas, and ran outside to look. And Mother jumped out of bed, and wrapped the down-quilt round Milly-Molly-Mandy, and went with her to the window to look (but there wasn't anything to see from there).

Then Father came back to say that one corner of the thatched roof was being blown off, and it would have to be seen to immediately before it got any worse. And then everybody began to get dressed.

Milly-Molly-Mandy thought it was kind of funny to have breakfast just the same as usual while the roof was blowing off. She felt very excited about it, and ate her porridge nearly all up before she even remembered beginning it!

"When shall you see to the roof?" asked Milly-Molly-Mandy. "Directly after breakfast?"

And Father said, "Yes, it must be seen to as soon as possible."

"How will you see to it?" asked Milly-Molly-Mandy. "With a long ladder?"

"And Father said, "No, it's too big a job for me. We must send to Mr Critch the Thatcher, and he'll bring a long ladder and mend it."

Milly-Molly-Mandy felt sorry that Father couldn't mend it himself, but it would be nice to see Mr Critch the Thatcher mend it.

Directly after breakfast Aunty put on her hat and coat to go down to the village with the message; and Milly-Molly-Mandy put on her hat and coat and went with her, because she wanted to see where Mr Critch the Thatcher lived. And as they went out of the gate the wind got another bit of thatch loose on the roof, and blew it down at them; so they hurried as fast as they could, along the white road with the hedges each side, down to the village.

But when Aunty knocked at Mr Critch the Thatcher's door (he lived in one of the little cottages just by the pond where the ducks were), Mrs Critch, the Thatcher's wife, opened it (and her apron blew about like a flag, it was so windy).

And Mrs Critch, the Thatcher's wife, said she was very sorry, but Mr Critch had just gone off in a hurry to mend another roof, and she knew he would not be able to come to them for a couple of days at the earliest, because he was so rushed – "what with this wind and all," said Mrs Critch.

"Dear, dear!" said Aunty. "Whatever shall we do?"

Mrs Critch was sorry, but she did not know what they could do, except wait until Mr Critch could come.

"Dear, dear!" said Aunty. "And meantime our roof will be getting worse and worse." Then Aunty and Milly-Molly-Mandy said good morning to Mrs Critch, and went out through her little gate into the road again.

"Father will have to mend it now, won't he, Aunty?" said Milly-Molly-Mandy.

"It isn't at all easy to thatch a roof," said Aunty. "You have to know how. I wonder what we can do!"

They set off back home along the white road with the hedges each side, and Aunty said, "Well, there must be a way out, somehow." And Milly-Molly-Mandy said, "I expect Father will know what to do."

So they hurried along, holding their hats on.

As they passed the Moggs's cottage they saw

little-friend-Susan trying to hang a towel on the line, with the wind trying all the time to wrap her up in it.

Milly-Molly-Mandy called out, "Hullo, Susan! Our roof's being blown off, and Mr Critch the Thatcher can't come and mend it, so Father will have to. Do you want to come and see?" Little-friend-Susan was very interested, and as soon as she had got the towel up she came along with them.

When Father and Mother and Grandpa and Grandma and Uncle heard their news they all looked as if they were saying, "Dear, dear!" to themselves. But Milly-Molly-Mandy looked quite pleased, and said, "Now you'll have to mend the roof, won't you Father?"

And Father looked at Uncle, and said, "Well, Joe. How about it?" And Uncle said, "Right, John!" in his big voice.

And then Father and Uncle buttoned their jackets (so that the wind shouldn't flap them), and fetched ladders (to reach the roof with), and a rake (to comb the straw tidy with), and wooden pegs (with which to fasten it down). And then they put one ladder so that they could climb up *to* the thatched roof, and another ladder with hooks on the end so that they could climb up *on* the thatched roof; and then Father gathered up a big armful of straw, and he and Uncle set to work busily to mend the hole in the thatch as well as they could, till Mr Critch the Thatcher could come.

Milly-Molly-Mandy and little-friend-Susan, down below, set to work busily to collect the straw from the hedges and the flower-beds and the grass, piling it up in one corner, ready for Father when he came down for another armful. And they helped to hold the ladder steady, and handed up sticks for making the pattern round the edge of the thatch, and fetched things that Father or Uncle called out for, and were very useful indeed.

Soon the roof began to look much better.

Then Father fetched a big pair of shears, and he snip-snip-snipped the straggly ends of the straw all round Milly-Molly-Mandy's little bedroom window up under the roof. (Milly-Molly-Mandy thought it was just like the nice white cottage having its hair cut!) And then Father and Uncle stretched a big piece of wire

Soon the roof began to look much better

netting over the mended place, and fastened it down with pegs. (Milly-Molly-Mandy thought it was just like the nice white cottage having a hair-net put on and fastened with hairpins!)

And then the roof was all trim and tidy again, and they wouldn't feel in any sort of a hurry for Mr Critch the Thatcher to come and thatch it properly.

"Isn't it a lovely roof?" said Milly-Molly-Mandy. "I knew Father could do it!"

"Well, you can generally manage to do a thing when you have to, Milly-Molly-Mandy," said Father, but he looked quite pleased with himself, and so did Uncle.

And when they saw what a nice snug roof they had now, so did Mother and Grandpa and Grandma and Aunty and Milly-Molly-Mandy!

19

MILLY-MOLLY-MANDY
KEEPS HOUSE

ONCE UPON A TIME Milly-Molly-Mandy
was left one evening in the nice white cottage
with the thatched roof to keep house.

There was something called a political meet-
ing being held in the next village (Milly-Molly-
Mandy didn't know quite what that meant, but
it was something to do with voting, which was
something you had to do when you grew up),
and Father and Mother and Grandpa and
Grandma and Uncle and Aunty all thought
they ought to go to it.

Milly-Molly-Mandy said she would not
mind one bit being left, especially if she could
have little-friend-Susan in to keep her company.

So Mother said, "Very well, then, Milly-
Molly-Mandy, we'll have little-friend-Susan in

181

to keep you company. And you needn't open the door if anyone knocks unless you know who it is. And I'll leave you out some supper, in case we may be a little late getting back."

Little-friend-Susan was only too pleased to come and spend the evening with Milly-Molly-Mandy. So after tea she came in; and then Father and Mother and Grandpa and Grandma and Uncle and Aunty put on their hats and coats, and said goodbye, and went off.

And Milly-Molly-Mandy and little-friend-Susan shut the door carefully after them, and there they were, all by themselves, keeping house!

"What fun!" said little-friend-Susan. "What'll we do?"

"Well," said Milly-Molly-Mandy, "if we're house-keepers I think we ought to wear aprons."

So they each tied on one of Mother's aprons.

And then little-friend-Susan said, "Now if we've got aprons on we ought to work."

So Milly-Molly-Mandy fetched a dustpan and brush and swept up some crumbs from the

floor; and little-friend-Susan folded the newspaper that was lying all anyhow by Grandpa's
chair and put it neatly on the shelf. And then
they banged the cushions and straightened the
chairs, feeling very housekeeperish indeed.

Then little-friend-Susan looked at the plates

of bread-and-dripping on the table, with the
jug of milk and two little mugs. And she said,
"What's that for?"

And Milly-Molly-Mandy said, "That's for

our supper. But it isn't time to eat it yet, Mother says we can warm the milk on the stove, if we like, in a saucepan."

"What fun!" said little-friend-Susan. "Then we'll be cooks. Couldn't we do something to the bread-and-dripping too?"

So Milly-Molly-Mandy looked at the bread-and-dripping thoughtfully, and then she said, "We could toast it – at the fire!"

"Oh, yes!" said little-friend-Susan. And then she said, "Oughtn't we to begin doing it now? It takes quite a long time to cook things."

So Milly-Molly-Mandy said, "Let's!" and fetched a saucepan, and little-friend-Susan took up the jug of milk, and then – suddenly – "Bang-bang-*bang*!" went the door knocker, ever so loudly.

"Ooh!" said little-friend-Susan, "that did make me jump! I wonder who it is!"

"Ooh!" said Milly-Molly-Mandy. "We mustn't open the door unless we know. I wonder who it can be!"

So together they went to the door, and Milly-Molly-Mandy put her mouth to the letter-box and said politely, "Please, who are you, please?"

Nobody spoke for a moment; and then a funny sort of voice outside said very gruffly, "I'm Mr Snooks."

And directly they heard that Milly-Molly-Mandy and little-friend-Susan looked at each other and said both together – "It's Billy Blunt!" And they unlocked the door and pulled it open.

And there was Billy Blunt standing grinning on the doorstep!

Milly-Molly-Mandy held the door wide for him to come in, and she said, "Did you think we didn't know you?"

And little-friend-Susan said, "You did give us a jump!" And Billy Blunt came in, grinning all over his face.

"We're all alone," said Milly-Molly-Mandy.

"We're keeping house."

"Look at our aprons," said little-friend-Susan. "We're going to cook our suppers."

"Come on," said Milly-Molly-Mandy, "and we'll give you some. May you stop?"

Billy Blunt let them pull him into the kitchen, and then he said he'd seen Father and Mother and Grandpa and Grandma and Uncle and Aunty as they went past the corn-shop to the crossroads, and Mother had told him they were alone, and that he could go and have a game with them if he liked. So he thought he'd come and give them a jump.

"Take your coat off, because it's hot in here," said Milly-Molly-Mandy. "Now we must get on with the cooking. Come on, Susan!"

So they put the milk into the saucepan on the back of the stove, and then they each took a piece of bread-and-dripping on a fork, to toast it.

But it wasn't a very good "toasting fire" (or else there were too many people trying to toast at the same time). Billy Blunt began to think it was rather long to wait, and he looked at the frying-pan on the side of the stove (in which

Mother always cooked the breakfast bacon), and said, "Why not put 'em in there and fry 'em up?"

Milly-Molly-Mandy and little-friend-Susan thought that was a splendid idea; so they fried all the bread-and-dripping nice and brown (and it did smell good!). When they had done it there was just a little fat left in the pan, so they looked round for something else to cook.

"I'll go and see if there're any odd bits of bread in the bread-crock," said Milly-Molly-Mandy. "We mustn't cut any, because I'm not allowed to use the bread-knife yet."

So she went into the scullery to look, and there were one or two dry pieces in the bread-crock. But she found something else, and that was – a big basket of onions! Then Milly-Molly-Mandy gave a little squeal because she had a good idea, and she took out a small onion (she knew she might, because they had lots, and Father grew them) and ran back into the kitchen with it.

And Billy Blunt, with his scout's knife, peeled it and sliced it into the pan (and the onion made him cry like anything!); and then

187

And the onions smelt most delicious!

Milly-Molly-Mandy fried it on the stove (and the onion made her cry like anything!) and then little-friend-Susan, who didn't want to be out of any fun stirred it up, with her head well over the pan (and the onion made her cry like anything too! – at least, she managed to get one small tear out).

And the onion smelt most delicious, all over the kitchen – only it would seem to cook all black or else not at all. But you can't think how good it tasted, spread on slices of fried bread!

They all sat on the hearthrug before the fire, with plates on their laps and mugs by their sides, and divided everything as evenly as possible. And they only wished there was more of everything (for of course Mother hadn't thought of Billy Blunt when she cut the bread-and-dripping).

When they had just finished the last crumb the door opened and Father and Mother and Grandpa and Grandma and Uncle and Aunty came in. And they all said together, "Whatever's all this smell of fried onions?"

So Milly-Molly-Mandy explained, and when

Mother had looked at the frying-pan to see that it wasn't burnt (and it wasn't) she only laughed and opened the window.

And Father said, "Well, this smell makes me feel very hungry. Can't we have some fried onions for supper too, Mother?"

Then, before Father took little-friend-Susan and Billy Blunt home, Mother gave them all a piece of currant cake with which to finish their supper; and then she started frying a panful of onions for the grown-up supper.

And Milly-Molly-Mandy (when she had said goodbye to little-friend-Susan and Billy Blunt) watched Mother very carefully, so that she should know how to fry quite properly next time she was left to keep house!

20

MILLY-MOLLY-MANDY AND THE BLACKSMITH'S WEDDING

ONCE UPON A TIME Milly-Molly-Mandy was going to a wedding.

It wasn't just the ordinary sort of wedding, where you stared through the churchyard railings, wondering at ladies walking outdoors in their party clothes and who the man in the tight collar was.

This was a very important wedding indeed.

Mr Rudge the Blacksmith was marrying the young lady who helped in Mrs Hubble the Baker's shop. And (which Milly-Molly-Mandy thought was the most important part) there were to be two bridesmaids. And the bridesmaids were Milly-Molly-Mandy and little-friend-Susan.

Milly-Molly-Mandy was sorry that Billy Blunt couldn't be a bridesmaid too, but Billy Blunt said he didn't care because he thought the most important part came later.

In the Village, in olden days, when the blacksmith or any of his family got married, he used to "fire the anvil" outside his forge, with real gunpowder, to celebrate! That's what Mr Rudge the Blacksmith said. He said his father had been married that way, and his uncle, and both his aunts, and his grandpa, and his great-grandpa a long time back. And that was how he meant to be married too, quite properly.

Billy Blunt didn't think many blacksmiths could be properly married, for he had never seen a blacksmith's wedding before, nor even heard one, and neither had Milly-Molly-Mandy, nor little-friend-Susan.

Anyhow, though he wasn't a bridesmaid, Billy Blunt had a proper invitation to the wedding, like Mr and Mrs Blunt (Billy Blunt's father and mother), and Mr and Mrs Moggs (little-friend-Susan's father and mother), and Milly-Molly-Mandy's Father and Mother and Grandpa and Grandma and Uncle and Aunty, and some other important friends. (For, of course, only important friends get proper invitations to weddings; the other sort have to peep through the railings or hang round by the lane.)

Well, it was only a few days to the wedding now, and Milly-Molly-Mandy and little-friend-Susan and Billy Blunt were coming home from afternoon school. And when they came to the corn-shop (where Billy Blunt lived) they could hear *clink-clang* noises coming from the Forge near by; so they all went round by the lane to have a look in. (For nobody can pass near a forge when things are going on without wanting to look in.)

Mr Rudge the Blacksmith was mending a plough, which wasn't quite so interesting to watch as shoeing a horse, but there was a nice piece of red-hot metal being hammered and bent to the right shape. The great iron hammer bounced off each time, as if it knew just how hot the metal was and didn't want to stay there long, and the iron anvil rang so loudly at every bang and bounce that the Blacksmith couldn't hear anyone speak. But presently he turned and buried the metal in his fire to heat it again, and the Blacksmith's Boy began working the handle of the bellows up and down till the flames roared and sparks flew.

It was just quiet enough then for Milly-Molly-Mandy to call out:

"Hello, Mr Rudge."

And Mr Rudge said, "Hello, there! Been turned out of school again, have you? Go on, Reginald, push her up."

So the boy pushed harder at the handle, and the fire roared and the sparks flew.

"Is that really his name?" asked Milly-Molly-Mandy.

"My name's Tom," said the boy, pumping away.

"Can't have two Toms here," said the Blacksmith. "That's my name. He'll have to be content with Reginald. Now then, out of the way, there!"

They all scattered in a hurry as the Blacksmith brought the piece of metal glowing hot out of the fire with his long-handled tongs, and laid it on the anvil again, and began to drill screw-holes in it. The drill seemed to go through the red-hot iron as easily as if it were cheese. As it cooled off and turned grey and hard again, the Blacksmith put it back into the fire. So then they could talk some more.

"Where do you put the gunpowder when you fire the anvil?" asked Billy Blunt.

"In that hole there," said the Blacksmith, pointing at his anvil.

So Billy Blunt and Milly-Molly-Mandy and little-friend-Susan bent over to see. And, sure enough, there was a small square hole in the top of the anvil. (You look at an anvil if you get the chance, and see.)

"That won't hold very much," said little-friend-Susan, quite disappointed.

"It'll hold a famous big bang – you wait," said the Blacksmith. "You don't want me to blow up all the lot of you, do you?"

"Have you got the gunpowder ready?" asked Milly-Molly-Mandy.

"I have," said Mr Rudge.

"Where do you keep it?" asked little-friend-Susan, looking about.

"Not just around here, I can tell you that much," said Mr Rudge.

"Where do you get the gunpowder?" asked Billy Blunt.

But the Blacksmith said he wasn't giving away any secrets like that. And he brought the piece of metal out of the fire and started hammering again.

When he had put it back into the fire Milly-Molly-Mandy said:

"Aunty has nearly finished making our bridesmaids' dresses, Mr Rudge."

"I should hope so!" said the Blacksmith. "How do you suppose I'm to be married next Saturday if you bridesmaids aren't ready? Go on, Reginald, get a move on."

"They're long dresses, almost down to our feet," said little-friend-Susan. "But we're to have a lot of tucks put in them afterwards, so that we can wear them for Sunday-best. And when we grow the tucks can be let out."

"That's an idea," said the Blacksmith. "I'll ask for tucks to be put in my wedding suit, so that I can wear it for Sunday-best afterwards."

Whereupon the Blacksmith's Boy burst out laughing so loudly, as he worked the bellows, that he made more noise than the other three all put together.

The Blacksmith fished the red-hot metal from the fire, and plunged it for a second into a tank of water near by, and there was a great hissing and steaming, and a lot of queer smell.

"What do you do that for?" asked Billy Blunt.

"Tempers the iron," said the Blacksmith,

trying it against the plough to see if it fitted properly; "brisks it up, like when you have a cold bath on a hot day."

He laid it on the anvil, and took up a smaller hammer and began tapping away. So Milly-Molly-Mandy and little-friend-Susan and Billy Blunt thought perhaps it was time to go now, so they said goodbye and went off home to their teas.

And Milly-Molly-Mandy and little-friend-Susan had another trying-on of their brides-maids' dresses after tea. And Aunty stitched and stitched away, so that they should be ready in time for the wedding.

Well, the great day came. And Milly-Molly-Mandy and little-friend-Susan, dressed alike in long pink dresses with bunches of roses in their hands, followed the young lady who helped Mrs Hubble the Baker, up the aisle of the church, to where Mr Rudge the Blacksmith was waiting.

Mr Rudge looked so clean in his new navy blue suit with shiny white collar and cuffs and a big white button-hole, that Milly-Molly-Mandy hardly knew him (though she had seen him clean before, when he played cricket on the playing-field, or walked out with the young lady who helped Mrs Hubble the Baker).

Then, when the marrying was done, Milly-Molly-Mandy and little-friend-Susan followed the Bride and Bridegroom down the aisle to the door, while everybody in the pews smiled and smiled, and Miss Bloss, who played the harmonium behind a red curtain, played so loudly and cheerfully, and Reginald the Blacksmith's Boy who pumped the bellows for her (so he did a lot of pumping one way and another) pushed the handle up and down so vigorously, it's a wonder they didn't burst the harmonium between them. (But they didn't often have a wedding to play for.)

Then the two Bridesmaids, with the Bride and Bridegroom, of course, stood outside on the church step to be photographed.

Then everybody walked in a procession down the lane, past the Blacksmith's house and past the Forge (which was closed), and up the road to the Inn, where a room had been hired

They stood on the church step to be photographed

for the wedding-breakfast (though it was early afternoon).

And then everybody stood around eating and drinking and making jokes and laughing and making speeches and clapping and laughing a lot more.

And Milly-Molly-Mandy and little-friend-Susan and Billy Blunt ate and laughed and clapped as much as anyone (though I'm not sure if Billy Blunt laughed as much as the others, as he was so busy "sampling" things).

They had two ice-creams each (as Grandma and one or two others didn't want theirs), and they had a big slice of wedding cake each, as well as helpings of nearly everything else, because Mr Rudge insisted on their having it, though their mothers said they'd had quite enough. (He was a very nice man!)

And then came the great moment when everybody came out of the Inn and went to the Forge to fire the anvil.

Mr Rudge unlocked the big doors and fastened them back. And then he and Father and Uncle and Mr Blunt and Mr Smale the Grocer between them pulled and pushed the heavy anvil outside into the lane. (The anvil had been cleaned up specially, so it didn't make their hands as dirty as you might think.)

And then Mr Rudge put some black powder into the little square hole in the anvil (Billy Blunt didn't see where he got it from). And the men-folk arranged a long piece of cord (which they called the fuse) from the hole down on to the ground. And then Mr Rudge took a box of matches from his pocket, and struck one, and set the end of the fuse alight.

And then everybody ran back and made a big half-circle round the front of the Forge and waited.

Mother and Mrs Moggs and Mrs Blunt wanted Milly-Molly-Mandy and little-friend-Susan and Billy Blunt to keep near them, and Mr Rudge kept by the young lady who used to help Mrs Hubble the Baker (but she wasn't going to any more, as she was Mrs Rudge now, and Mr Rudge said she'd have her work cut out looking after him). She seemed very fright-ened and held her hands over her ears, so he kept his arm round her.

Milly-Molly-Mandy and little-friend-Susan

put their hands half over their ears and hopped up and down excitedly. But Billy Blunt put his hands in his pockets and stood quite still. He said he didn't want to waste any of the bang.

The little flame crept along the fuse, nearer and nearer. And it began to creep up the anvil. And they all waited, breathless, for the big bang. They waited. And they waited.

And they waited.

"What's the matter with the thing?" said Mr Rudge, taking his arm away from the young lady who was Mrs Rudge now. "Has the fuse gone out? Keep back, everybody, it isn't safe yet."

So they waited some more. But still nothing happened.

At last Mr Rudge walked over to the anvil, and so did the other men (though the women didn't want them to).

"Ha!" said Mr Rudge. "Fuse went out just as it reached the edge of the anvil. Now what'll we do? It's too short to re-light."

"I've got some string," said Billy Blunt, and he rummaged in his breeches pocket.

"Bring it here, and let's have a look at it," said Mr Rudge.

So Billy Blunt went close and gave it to him (and took a good look into the hole at the same time).

"Will that carry the flame, d'you think?" said Father.

"Might do, if you give it a rub with a bit of candle-wax," said Mr Smale the Grocer.

"I think I've got a bit of wax," said Billy Blunt, rummaging in his pocket again.

"Hand it over," said Mr Rudge. "What else have you got in there – a general store?"

"It's bees-wax, not candle-wax, though," said Billy Blunt.

"Never mind, so long as it's wax," said Mr Blunt.

"It's got a bit stuck," said Billy Blunt, still rummaging.

"You boys – whatever will you put in your pockets next?" said Mrs Blunt.

"Better turn it inside out," said Uncle

So Billy Blunt pulled his whole pocket outside. And there *were* a lot of things in it – marbles, and horse-chestnuts, and putty, and a pocket-knife, and a pencil-holder, and a broken key, and a ha'penny, and several bus tickets, and some other things. And stuck half into the lining at the seam was a lump of bees-wax, which they dug off with the pocket-knife.

"You have your uses, William," said Mr Rudge. And he waxed the string, and arranged it to hang from the anvil along the ground. And he struck a match and lit the end. And everybody ran back again in a hurry, and made a big half-circle round the anvil, and waited as before.

And the little flame crept along, and it paused and looked as if it were going out, and it crept on again, and it reached the anvil, and it began to creep up, and everybody waited, and Milly-Molly-Mandy and little-friend-Susan put their hands over their ears and smiled at each other, and Billy Blunt put his hands deep in his pockets and frowned straight ahead.

And the little flame crept up the string to the top of the anvil, and everybody held their breath, and Milly-Molly-Mandy pressed her hands hard over her ears, and then she was afraid she might not hear enough so she lifted them off – and, just at that very moment, there came a great big enormous B A N G!

And Milly-Molly-Mandy and little-friend-Susan jumped and gave a shriek because they were so splendidly startled (even though they were expecting it). And Billy Blunt grinned and looked pleased. And everybody began to talk and exclaim together as they went forward to look at the anvil (which wasn't hurt at all, only a bit dirty-looking round the hole).

Then everybody shook hands with the Blacksmith and his Bride, and told them they certainly had been properly married, and wished them well. And the Blacksmith

thanked them all
heartily.

And when it
came time for
Milly-Molly-
Mandy and lit-
tle-friend-Susan
and Billy Blunt
to shake hands
and say thank-you-for-
a-nice-wedding-party, Mr Rudge said:

"Well, now, what sort of a wedding it would
have been without you bridesmaids, and Billy
Blunt to provide all our requirements out of
his ample pockets, I just cannot conceive!"

And everybody laughed, and Mr Rudge
smacked Billy Blunt on the shoulder so that he
nearly fell over (but it didn't hurt him).

So then Milly-Molly-Mandy and little-
friend-Susan and Billy Blunt each knew that
they had been very important indeed in helping to give Mr Rudge a really proper
Blacksmith's Wedding!

21

MILLY-MOLLY-MANDY
HAS A NEW DRESS

ONCE UPON A TIME Milly-Molly-Mandy was playing hide-and-seek with Toby the dog.

First Milly-Molly-Mandy threw a stone as far as she could, and then while Toby the dog was fetching it Milly-Molly-Mandy ran the other way and hid in among the gooseberry and currant bushes or behind the wall. And then Toby the dog came to look for her. He was so clever he always found her almost at once – even when she hid in the stable where Twinkletoes the pony lived (only he was out in the meadow eating grass now).

She shut the lower half of the stable door and kept quite quiet, but Toby the dog barked and scratched outside, and wouldn't go away till Milly-Molly-Mandy pushed open the door and came out.

Then Toby the dog was so pleased to see her, and so pleased with himself for finding her, that he jumped up and down on his hind legs, pawing and scratching at her skirt.

And suddenly – rrrrrip! – there was a great big tear all the way down the front of Milly-Molly-Mandy's pink-and-white striped cotton frock.

"Oh dear, oh dear!" said Milly-Molly-

Mandy. "Oh, Toby, just see what you've done now!"

Then Toby the dog stopped jumping up and down, and he looked very sorry and ashamed of himself. So Milly-Molly-Mandy said, "All right, then! Poor Toby! You didn't mean to do it. But whatever will Mother say? I'll have to go and show her."

So Milly-Molly-Mandy, looking very solemn and holding her dress together with both hands, walked back through the barnyard where the cows were milked (only they, too, were out in the meadow eating grass now).

Uncle was throwing big buckets of water over the floor of the cowshed, to wash it. "Now what have you been up to?" he asked, as Milly-Molly-Mandy, looking very solemn and holding her dress together with both hands, passed by.

"I tore my dress playing with Toby, and I'm going to show Mother," said Milly-Molly-Mandy.

"Well, well," said Uncle, sending another big bucketful of water swashing along over the brick floor. "Now you'll catch it. Tell Mother to send you out to me if she wants you to get a good spanking. I'll give you a proper one!"

"Mother won't let you spank me!" said Milly-Molly-Mandy (she knew Uncle was only joking). "But she won't like having to mend such a great big tear, I expect. She mended this dress only a little while ago, and now it's got to be done all over again. Come on, Toby."

So they went through the gate into the kitchen garden (where Father grew the vegetables) and in by the back door of the nice white cottage with the thatched roof where Father and Mother and Grandpa and Grandma and Uncle and Aunty and, of course, Milly-Molly-Mandy all lived together.

"Now what's the matter with little Millicent Margaret Amanda?" said Grandma, who was shelling peas for dinner, as Milly-Molly-Mandy came in, looking very solemn and holding her dress together with both hands.

"I'm looking for Mother," said Milly-Molly-Mandy.

"She's in the larder," said Aunty, who was patching sheets with her machine at the kitchen table. "What have you been up to?"

But Milly-Molly-Mandy went over to the door of the larder, where Mother was washing the shelves.

"Mother," said Milly-Molly-Mandy, looking

very solemn and holding her dress together with both hands, "I'm dreadfully sorry, but I was playing hide-and-seek with Toby, and we tore my dress. Badly."

"Dear, dear, now!" said Grandma.

"Whatever next!" said Aunty.

"Let me have a look," said Mother. She put down her wash-cloth and came out into the kitchen.

Milly-Molly-Mandy took her hands away and showed her frock, with the great big tear all down the front of it.

Mother looked at it. And then she said:

"Well, Milly-Molly-Mandy! That just about finishes that frock! But I was afraid it couldn't last much longer when I mended it before."

And Grandma said, "She had really out-grown it."

And Aunty said, "It was very faded."

And Mother said, "You will have to have a new one."

Milly-Molly-Mandy was pleased to think that was all they said about it. (So was Toby the dog!)

Mother said, "You can go out in the garden and tear it all you like now, Milly-Molly-Mandy. But don't you go tearing anything else!"

So Milly-Molly-Mandy and Toby the dog had a fine time tearing her old dress to ribbons, so that she looked as if she had been

Milly-Molly-Mandy showed her dress with the tear all down the front

dancing in a furze bush, Grandpa said. And then Mother sent her upstairs to change into her better frock (which was pink-and-white striped, too).

During dinner Mother said, "I'm going to take Milly-Molly-Mandy down to the Village this afternoon, to buy her some stuff for a new dress."

Father said, "I suppose that means you want some more money." And he took some out of his trousers' pocket and handed it over to Mother.

Grandma said, "What about getting her something that isn't pink-and-white striped, just for a change?"

Grandpa said, "Let's have flowers instead of stripes this time."

Aunty said, "Something with daisies on would look nice."

Uncle said, "Oh, let's go gay while we are about it, and have magenta roses and yellow sunflowers – eh, Milly-Molly-Mandy?"

But Milly-Molly-Mandy said, "I don't 'spect Miss Muggins keeps that sort of stuff in her shop, so then I can't have it!"

After dinner Milly-Molly-Mandy helped Mother to wash up the plates and things, and then Mother changed her dress, and they put on their hats, and Mother took her handbag, and they went together down the road with the hedges each side towards the Village.

They passed the Moggs' cottage, where little-friend-Susan lived. Little-friend-Susan was helping her baby sister to make mud pies on the step.

"Hullo, Susan," said Milly-Molly-Mandy. "We're going to buy me some different new dress stuff at Miss Muggins' shop, because I tore my other one!"

"Are you? How nice! What colour are you going to have this time?" asked little-friend-Susan.

"We don't know yet, but it will be something quite different," said Milly-Molly-Mandy.

They passed the Forge, where Mr Rudge the Blacksmith and his new boy were making a big fire over an iron hoop which, when it was red-hot, they were going to fit round a broken cart-wheel to mend it. Milly-Molly-Mandy wanted to stay and watch, but Mother said she hadn't time.

So Milly-Molly-Mandy just called out to Mr Rudge, "We're going to buy some different-coloured dress stuff, because I tore my other one!"

And Mr Rudge stopped to wipe his hot face on his torn shirt sleeve, and said, "Well, if they'd buy us different-coloured shirts every time we tear ours, you'd see us going about like a couple of rainbows! Eh, Reginald?"

And the new boy grinned as he piled more brushwood on the fire. (He'd got a tear in his shirt too.)

They passed Mr Blunt's corn-shop, where Billy Blunt was polishing up his new second-hand bicycle, which his father had just given him, on the pavement outside.

Milly-Molly-Mandy and Mother stopped a minute to admire its shininess (which

was almost like new). And then Milly-Molly-Mandy said, "We're going to buy me some different-coloured dress stuff, because I tore my other!"

But Billy Blunt wasn't very interested (he was just testing his front brake).

Then they came to Miss Muggins' shop.

And just as they got up to the door so did two other people, coming from the other way. One was an old lady in a black cloak and bonnet, and one was a little girl in a faded flowered dress, with a ribbon round her hair. Mother pushed open the shop door for the old lady and set the little bell jangling above, and they all went in together, so that the shop seemed quite full of people, with Miss Muggins behind the counter too.

Miss Muggins didn't know quite whom to serve first. She looked towards the old lady, and the old lady looked towards Mother, and Mother said, "No, you first."

So then the old lady said, "I would like to see something for a dress for a little girl, if you please – something light and summery."

And Mother said, "That is exactly what I am

wanting, too.'

So then Miss Muggins brought out the different stuffs from her shelves for both her customers to choose from together.

Milly-Molly-Mandy looked at the little girl. She thought she had seen her before. Surely it was the new little girl who had lately come to Milly-Molly-Mandy's school. Only she was in the "baby class", so they hadn't talked together yet.

The little girl looked at Milly-Molly-Mandy. And presently she pulled at the old lady's arm and whispered something, whereupon the old lady turned and smiled at Milly-Molly-Mandy, so Milly-Molly-Mandy smiled back.

Milly-Molly-Mandy whispered up at Mother (looking at the little girl). "She comes to our school!"

So then Mother smiled at the little girl. And the old lady and Mother began to talk together as they looked at Miss Muggins' stuffs. And Milly-Molly-Mandy and the little girl began to talk too, as they waited.

Milly-Molly-Mandy found out that the little girl was called Bunchy, and the old lady was her grandmother, and they lived together in a little cottage quite a long way from the school and the crossroads, in the other direction from Milly-Molly-Mandy's.

Bunchy hadn't come to school before because she couldn't walk so far. But now she was bigger, and Granny walked with her half the way and she ran the rest by herself. She liked coming to school, but she had never played with other little girls and boys before, and it all felt very strange and rather frightening. So then Milly-Molly-Mandy said they should look out for each other at school next Monday, and play together during play-time. And she told her about little-friend-Susan, and Billy Blunt, and Miss Muggins' Jilly, and other friends at school.

Then Mother said to Miss Muggins, "And this is all you have in the way of printed cottons? Well, now, I wonder, Milly-Molly-

Mandy."

And Bunchy's Grandmother said, "Look here, Bunchy, my dear."

So they both went up to the counter.

There was a light blue silky stuff which Mother and Bunchy's Grandmother said was "not serviceable." And a stuff with scarlet poppies and corn- flowers all over it which they said was "not suitable". And there was a green chintz stuff which they said was too thick. And a yellow muslin which they said was too thin.  And there was a stuff with little bunches of daisies and forget-me-nots on it. And a big roll of pink-and-white striped cotton. And there was nothing more (except flannelette or bolton-sheeting and that sort of thing, which wouldn't do at all).

Milly-Molly-Mandy thought the one with daisies and forget-me-nots was much the prettiest. So did Bunchy. Milly-Molly-Mandy thought a dress of that would be a very nice change.

But Miss Muggins said, "I'm afraid I have only this short length left, and I don't know when I shall be having any more in."

So Mother and Bunchy's Grandmother spread it out, and there was really only just enough to make one little frock. Bunchy's Grandmother turned to look at the pink-and-white striped stuff.

Bunchy said, "That's Milly-Molly-Mandy's stuff, isn't it? It's just like the dress she has on."

Milly-Molly-Mandy said, "Do you always have flowers on your dresses?"

"Yes," said Bunchy, "because of my name, you know. I'm Violet Rosemary May, but Granny calls me Bunchy for short."

Milly-Molly-Mandy said to Mother, "She ought to have that stuff with the bunches of flowers on, oughtn't she? The striped one wouldn't really suit her so well as me, would it?"

Mother said, "Well, Milly-Molly-Mandy, we

do know this striped stuff suits you all right, and it washes and wears well. I'm afraid that blue silky stuff doesn't look as if it would wash, and the yellow muslin wouldn't wear. So perhaps you'd better have the same again. I'll take two yards of this striped, please, Miss Muggins."

Milly-Molly-Mandy looked once more at the flowery stuff, and she said, "It is pretty, isn't it! But if Bunchy comes to school I can see it on her, can't I?"

Bunchy's Grandmother said, "It would be very nice if you could come and see it on Bunchy at home too! If Mother would bring you to tea one Saturday, if you don't mind rather a walk, you could play in the garden with Bunchy, and I'm sure we should both be very pleased indeed, shouldn't we, Bunchy?"

Bunchy said, "Yes! We should!"

Mother said, "Thank you very much. We should like to come" – though she had not much time for going out to tea as a rule, but she was sure Aunty would get tea for them all at home for once.

So it was settled for them to go next

Saturday, and the little girl called Bunchy was very pleased indeed about it, and so was Milly-Molly-Mandy.

Then Miss Muggins handed over the counter the two parcels, and Milly-Molly-Mandy and Bunchy each carried her own dress stuff home.

And when Milly-Molly-Mandy opened her parcel to show Father and Grandpa and Grandma and Uncle and Aunty what had been bought for her new dress after all, there was a beautiful shiny red ribbon there too, which Mother had bought to tie round Milly-Molly-Mandy's hair when she wore the new dress. So that would make quite a nice change, anyhow.

And as little-friend-Susan said, if Milly-Molly-Mandy didn't wear her pink-and-white stripes peo-ple might not know her at once.

And that would be a pity!

The Nice White Cottage with the Thatched Roof (where Milly-Molly-Mandy lives)

The Meadow (where M·M·M and Billy Blunt practised racing)

The Barn (where M·M·M gave a party)

Brook

The Moggs's Cottage (where little-friend-Susan lives)

(only used in dry weather) Short cut to School

Woods

To Another Village

MAP of th